happily never after

happily never after

JENNIFER HONEYBOURN

For Dallas

"IT LOOKS GOOD, RIGHT?" my sister Laurel says. Her beaded turquoise chandelier earrings swing as she stuffs the last bunch of wildflowers we just picked from the garden into a burlap-wrapped mason jar.

We're in the apple orchard behind her soon-to-be in-law's house, checking out the setup before everyone is due to arrive for the welcome dinner, the official kick-off event for Laurel and Andrew's wedding weekend. The rustic wooden table is laid out with gleaming white dishes and polished silverware. Wine glasses engraved with Laurel and Andrew's initials entwined inside of a heart are at each place setting and fat white candles are evenly spaced down the length of the table. Fairy lights are strung in the trees and will cast a magical glow as soon as the sun goes down.

"It looks great," I reply. "Very rustic chic."

I can't help but cringe soon as the words leave my mouth. Rustic chic is Laurel's "wedding aesthetic". Against my own will, I've somehow become fluent in wedding slang. God, what is happening to me?

My sister smiles and grabs a violet from the jar. She tucks it into my braid crown, right above my ear. "There. Now you look rustic chic, too."

She squeezes my shoulders, bare in the blush pink maxi dress she insisted I wear for this dinner. I fake a smile. This dress is very much not my style, but she was so adamant I wear it that it was easier to just give in than to fight her on it.

I've been giving in a lot over the past six months. Thank god the big day is almost here. I'm so sick of talking about invitations and centerpieces and favors, sick of all of this over-the-top ridiculousness. Laurel spent almost five thousand dollars on a dress she's going to wear for one evening — a drop in the bucket compared to the total cost of this wedding — and I've kept my mouth shut about all of it, even though I really want to shake her and ask her why on earth she's decided to get married in the first place.

Laurel leans over the table to study the chalkboard place cards. She has such a need to control every detail that she's wasting time out here, fiddling over place cards, when she should be getting dressed for dinner — she's still in her white hoodie with Bride emblazoned in crystals on the back.

Her face darkens as she snatches up Dad and Rachel's cards. "Who moved these?" she asks, already walking the cards down to the opposite end of the table, far away from where the rest of my family has been assigned to sit.

"Arden, you have to keep Dad and Rachel away from mom," she calls over her shoulder.

I frown. Our parents have promised to be on their best behavior this weekend, but that really doesn't count for much. They made the same promise four years ago, for

Laurel's high school graduation, and that night ended with a huge screaming match in the school parking lot. I get that my sister is worried about how they'll behave, but I'm not sure how she expects me to control them. She might as well ask me to change the weather.

"How am I'm supposed to do that?"

"I don't care how you do it." Laurel plunks the place cards down in front of two seats at the very edge of the table, banishing Dad and his new wife to the fringes where she obviously thinks they both belong. "You just need to do it."

Okay, I get that this is her wedding and she wants everything to be perfect, but someone needs to tell her that perfect doesn't actually exist. Something is bound to go wrong at some point and I wish she would stop worrying about all the stupid details. But that's not Laurel. She lives for stupid details.

She straightens the burlap bow attached to the back of one of the wooden chairs that look like they've been made out of branches. "By the way, how is your speech coming along?" she asks.

A flash of guilt zips through me. My sister is adamant that I give a speech tonight, even though she knows I'm legit terrified of public speaking. Every time I think about standing up in front of everyone — even if they are just family and friends — I feel like I might throw up.

"Good," I squeak.

Laurel glares at me. My sister is stunning – strawberry-blonde hair, blue eyes, freckles lightly dusting the bridge of her perfect button nose. She could easily be on the cover of a bridal magazine, if she could only channel happiness and joy instead of anxiety and stress.

"You have written your speech, right?" she says, narrowing her eyes. "You know how important this is to me."

But that's the problem — everything about this wedding is important to her. Every. Single. Thing. It's completely taken over our lives. It's all she can talk about. She somehow manages to turn every conversation back to the topic of first dances and bouquets and fondant icing, like there aren't more important things going on in the world.

"Yes, I've written something," I lie. I know she's expecting me to deliver a speech that's meaningful and heartfelt, something that might even bring a tear to her eye, but that level of emotion is a million miles out of my comfort zone. I've been hoping that the right words would come to me some point, but they haven't. Giving a speech is a terrible idea, the *very worst idea*, and I can't believe that she's actually going to make me do it. "Um, I'm going to practice it now, actually," I add.

I must be a pretty good liar — either that or Laurel's too preoccupied with straightening the silverware to notice that I'm not meeting her eyes — because her shoulders relax slightly. "Okay, great." She studies the table one last time, nudging a knife into place, and then leaves to get dressed.

Once she's gone, all of the tension goes with her. I look around the orchard. It's so peaceful here — it really is a beautiful place to host a dinner. The heat of the day has finally loosened its grip and the air smells like wildflowers. Apple trees circle the grove, their branches heavy with red and green fruit. I would love to curl up under one of those trees, maybe read a book or take a nap. Instead, I'm stuck at this dinner, sandwiched between my mom and Andrew's ancient aunt Margaret.

Guess it'd better practice this speech. I sigh and pick up a fork, holding it in front of me like a microphone.

"Hi everyone," I start. "I'm Arden, Laurel's sister. I'm so honored to be part of this wedding." My stomach flips and my palms start to sweat, even though my audience is made up of imaginary people.

"I'm so glad that Laurel has found her prince charming," I say. "I'm sure that she and Andrew will have a very happy life together."

I make a face. This all sounds so generic and impersonal, like I could be talking about any couple, but the problem is, I don't know what to say about Laurel and Andrew because I haven't spent much time with them. I've only seen my sister a handful of times since she moved here to Toronto four years ago and the distance — along with the four years between us — has made things difficult. Almost everything I know about Laurel's life I learn from Instagram, so it came as a huge surprise when she asked me to be her maid of honor. Although truthfully I think that the only reason she chose me is because it was easier than trying to decide between her friends.

As for Andrew, all I really know about him is that he likes craft beer, fantasy football and he once went to Iceland. Oh, and he works in banking, something to do with mortgages. But I'm not sure how to spin any of that into a moving speech.

I clutch the fork a little tighter. "I knew that Andrew was special when Laurel brought him home to San Diego for Christmas a few years ago."

This is not true. I didn't think there was anything particularly special about Andrew when Laurel first introduced us and I certainly didn't think that we'd end up being related one day. Maybe if I had, I would have paid more attention to him.

"Um. It might seem like Andrew and Laurel are total opposites — she doesn't like fantasy football and he's not into restoring old furniture — but in the words of the great Ed Sheeran, people fall in love in mysterious ways." I wince and set the fork back down onto the table. This is perhaps the worst maid of honor speech in the history of ever. Laurel is going to kill me.

Maybe the reason it sounds so false is because I can't wrap my head around the fact that she even wants to get married. She's twenty-one, she *just* graduated college. Not to mention, something like fifty percent of marriages end in divorce — our parents are a statistic. If their divorce taught me anything, it's that there's no such thing as happily-ever-after. Eventually, people grow tired of each other. There's no way that I would ever take the risk — it just doesn't seem worth it. And up until recently I would have bet that my sister felt the same way.

A branch snaps. I'm startled as a tall blonde guy emerges from behind the trees, a big, black dog following at his heels, its long pink tongue hanging out of its slobbery mouth. Before I know what's happening, the dog bounds across the grass and jumps on me, pinning me against the table, straining to try and lick my face.

"Percy!" the guy yells. He runs over and yanks the dog off me by the collar. "Oh god, I'm so sorry. He's friendly, I promise."

"Maybe a little too friendly," I say, wiping dog slobber off my neck.

"You must be Arden," he says. He's wearing a black t-shirt and blue athletic shorts with high top sneakers. "I'm Shep. Andrew's brother."

I swallow. I knew that Andrew had a younger brother, but I did not expect him to look like this. Andrew's handsome, in a Ken-doll sort of way, so I guess I figured that his brother would be cast from the same generically good-looking mold, but their physical similarities end with their dark blonde hair. Shep is taller and leaner. His brown eyes are set underneath thick eyebrows and he hasn't quite grown into his nose yet. His hands are large and currently engaged with trying to keep his dog from leaping onto me again.

"For what it's worth, I think your speech is great," he adds.

"It's not, but past me decided to leave it to the last minute," I say. "I thought it would be more spontaneous and in-the-moment that way. But, as it turns out, past me was very wrong. Past me has royally screwed over present me."

Shep smiles and my heart begins to pick up speed. He's super cute, exactly the type of guy I'd go for, if I was interested in getting up to no good this weekend. Which I'm not.

"Well, I could help you if you like," he says, just as Laurel hollers for me from the house.

I sigh. "Duty calls."

"That's exactly why I've been hiding out all afternoon,"

he says. He motions for his dog to follow him and they melt back into the trees. I take a deep breath and head up the bark chip path, wishing that I could disappear, too.

two

WHEN I GET up to the house, Laurel is nowhere to be seen. The other bridesmaids are by the bar, already indulging in the free champagne. Nathalie and Charlotte are chatting up the bartender, a lantern-jawed guy with a man bun. Riya stands slightly apart from them, a bored expression on her face. She catches my eye and smiles.

I begged Laurel to let Riya give the speech — she's a theatre major! She's used to being in front of a crowd — but my sister insisted that, as the maid of honor, I have to do it. I guess I should just be grateful that she's agreed to let me do it tonight instead of at the actual wedding, when hundreds of people would be staring at me.

"Hi, Arden," Riya says. She's wearing a yellow peasant dress that swirls around her knees and an armful of wooden bangles that knock together every time she moves. Her dark hair is super short, a sore point with Laurel, who wanted her to grow it out or get extensions for the wedding. I don't know Riya very well but I like her for not giving in to my sister's ridiculous demands. And I wish I had her balls. Maybe if I did, I wouldn't be stuck wearing a dress I hate.

"Your dad's here," she adds.

Well, now I know why Laurel summoned me. The other guests aren't actually supposed to arrive for another forty-five minutes, but for some reason, Dad's decided to show up early.

"I guess I'd better go find him," I say.

I head into the house, following the sound of Dad's booming laugh. He's with Rachel in the front hall, making small talk with Mrs. Tremblay, Andrew's mother. His eyes light up when he sees me coming towards them.

"Ardie! I've missed you." He grabs me in a bear hug and squeezes a little too hard.

"I just saw you last week," I say, patting him on the back. "Also, you're early."

"We wanted to spend some time with you and your sister before everyone else got here," he says.

"Everyone else" is code for my mom. Unfortunately for my dad, she's already somewhere in the house, probably hiding from him and his new wife.

Speaking of...

"Hi Rachel," I say.

Rachel smiles. "You look beautiful. Pink is your color."

It's really not, but she's trying to be nice, so I smile back at her. Rachel tucks a strand of her long silver hair behind her ear. She and my dad work in the same law firm. They're both divorce lawyers. My mom and Laurel refuse to believe there wasn't anything going on between them while my mom was still married to my dad, even though he didn't actually start dating Rachel until a year after my parents split.

"Arden, honey, why don't you get your dad and Rachel a drink and then take them down to see the orchard?" Mrs. Tremblay says, fiddling with one of her pearl earrings. It's a signal — keep them out of the house and far away from your sister and mother.

My stomach sinks. Dinner isn't for another hour. I know she's just carrying out Laurel's orders but separating my dad and Rachel from the rest of the guests feels wrong. Fortunately, they don't seem to register what's happening and they happily follow me through the house.

I usher them past the kitchen, which is filled with catering staff and smells like roast chicken, and onto the deck. Riya, Nathalie and Charlotte have disappeared, which is great because if my dad saw them then he'd want to talk to them and then we'd never get out of there. Once my dad starts talking it's almost impossible to drag him away from a conversation.

We make a pit-stop at the bar so he can order a vodka soda. Rachel and I opt for sparkling water.

"So, Ardie," Dad says, as we continue down to the orchard. "Thought anymore about Maryland?"

I grimace. Oh god, not now.

"Not really," I say, hoping he'll drop the subject. He's been after me to apply to The University of Maryland, his alma mater. He wants me to go to a good pre-law school, just in case I decide that I want to follow in his footsteps. That will never happen. I have no interest in becoming a lawyer — I'm going to major in classical studies so I can teach Greek mythology, maybe do an academic exchange and spend a semester or two at the University of Thessaloniki in Athens — but he keeps hoping I'll change my mind.

This all loops back to Laurel. She'd always talked about going into law — it was the plan — but that was before my parents' relationship went south. After the divorce, my sister swung in a completely different direction. She moved to Toronto to study at the Ontario College of Art and Design and although she swears that the divorce had nothing to do with her decision, I'm pretty sure not going to law school was a big middle finger to our dad.

"I thought we could take a trip to the campus," Dad says. "Maybe go to homecoming. I'd love to show you around."

"Maybe."

The trees part and we reach the clearing. Rachel scans the table for their place cards. When she finally locates them, way down at the end of the table, she frowns. She and my dad exchange a glance that seems weighted with meaning, but neither of them says a word. My face burns and I feel guilty, even though none of this is my fault.

I set my glass down in front of my own place card. I glance at the card to my left, where Andrew's Aunt Margaret is supposed to sit, only now I see Shep's name written in black cursive.

My heart pounds. He must have switched the place cards. He wants to sit beside me. I mean, I know we had a moment earlier, but this is a pretty clear statement that he wants to get to know me better.

Nervous anticipation sweeps through me. Laurel is going to freak when she notices the cards have been switched. I consider switching them back — my sister spent hours working on the seating arrangements for all of the events this weekend — but the truth is, the night is bound to be more interesting if I sit beside Shep instead of Aunt Margaret, so I decide not to change them.

Since there's not a lot to do while we wait for everyone else to get here, I walk over to Dad and Rachel. Rachel makes several attempts to engage me in conversation — how was your flight? (fine), are you looking forward to your senior year? (yes), have you seen any good movies lately (nope) — but I'm too distracted to give her more than one-word answers. My nerves are off-the-charts. I can't think about anything right now except my speech. The one I still haven't written. The one I'm supposed to deliver in less than an hour.

Dad is uncharacteristically quiet. He knocks back his drink and drums his fingers on the table. Rachel reaches over to still his hand and he gives her a small smile. I glance away from them, a surge of anger coursing through me. I always end up defaulting to rage when I'm around them for longer than a few minutes. It's just so obvious that my dad's much happier with Rachel than he was with my mom and it's hard not to feel resentful. He seems like a completely different person with her — calmer, more relaxed and a lot more patient. That all goes out the window when he's around my mother.

Half an hour later, long after we've run out of things to say to each other, I wander back to my seat at the other end of the table just as the fiddler Laurel hired arrives. He has a handlebar moustache and he's wearing red suspenders, like he's time-travelled here from the 1800s. He nods at me and starts to play a folksy song, stamping one of his feet in time to the music, as people start to filter into the orchard.

One of those people is Shep.

"Hey," he says, plunking down beside me. He's traded his t-shirt and shorts for a neatly pressed white button up shirt and khaki pants. His dark blonde hair is still artfully messy, falling casually over one brown eye. "I switched the place cards."

"I noticed."

He grins. "Do you think Laurel is trying to keep us apart on purpose?"

Despite myself, I smile back. I already like Shep, but if experience has taught me anything, it's that these things always end badly. Also, he's about to become Laurel's brother-in-law, so I know without even asking that she'd consider him completely off-limits.

Before I can reply, my mom enters the orchard, clutching the arm of Andrew's uncle, her loud laugher interrupting all conversation. She makes a point of enthusiastically greeting everyone at the table except for Dad and Rachel and sits down in the empty chair beside me.

Laurel and Andrew are right behind her. My sister is smiling but it doesn't quite reach her eyes. When she spots Shep sitting where he's not supposed to be sitting, her mouth tightens. She makes a move to walk over to us, but Andrew says something to her and she stops. He nuzzles her neck with his nose and to my amazement, she softens.

"Ready for your big speech?" Shep asks me.

I shake my head, my stomach plunging. I feel myself starting to panic. I keep hoping the right words will magically come to me, but so far, I've got nothing and I'm running out of time.

Maybe alcohol will help, I think. It's supposed to loosen you up, right? When my mom looks in the other direction, I grab one of the wine bottles from the centre of the table and slosh some red wine into my glass.

"Well, being nervous about public speaking is normal," Shep says.

"I'm way past nervous," I reply, taking a sip of wine. I wrinkle my nose at the bitter taste. Yuck, why do people drink this stuff? "I just want to get through it without throwing up. I still have no idea what to say."

Shep stands. "Come with me."

"I think they're about to serve dinner."

"We'll be back before anyone even notices we're gone," he says.

Laurel will notice. She may not be watching us now, but there's no way it will escape her attention that we're not at the table. I'm going to hear about this later, for sure.

But I grab the bottle of wine — gross or not, I need it — and follow Shep into the trees.

We walk through the orchard for a minute or so until we reach a wooden gazebo covered in lacy green vines. The sun hasn't fully set yet and there's just enough light to see the stone bench inside. We sit down and I take a long slug of wine. Funny thing — the more I drink, the better it tastes.

"I come here all the time when I need a minute," he says.

"I can see why." This place is a refuge. I can still hear laughter and music, but it's muffled by the trees, far enough away that it's easy to feel like we're totally alone.

"I thought it might help to just get away from every-thing," he says."When you stand up to give your speech, take a deep breath. And remember to picture everyone naked."

I laugh. "Even your great-aunt Margaret?"

He wrinkles his nose. "Well, maybe not her." He grins and something inside of me lights up. I quickly push those feelings down — no good can come from them — and shift away from him, putting a bit more space between us.

"Just speak from the heart," he adds.

Maybe it's Shep or maybe it's the alcohol kicking in— either way, I'm feeling calm and relaxed.

I'm making way too much out of this speech. It's two minutes of my life. No one will even remember what I say. I'll just talk about how Laurel and Andrew are the perfect couple, true love forever, blah blah blah. I don't have to mean it, I just have to act like I do.

It'll be fine.

"So. If my brother is marrying your sister, does that makes us family?" Shep asks me as I pass him the wine bottle.

I frown. "I don't think so."

"Good," he says, giving me a sly smile. He takes a drink of wine just as Riya comes through the trees.

"There you are! Laurel is having a fit. You guys better come back to the table."

"It's all my fault," Shep says. "I convinced Arden to run away with me."

Riya shakes her head but when he looks the other way, she widens her eyes at me. "Cute," she mouths.

I nudge her with my elbow.

The food is already on the table when we arrive back at the party — big wooden bowls of coleslaw and wicker baskets of freshly-baked buns, platters of roast chicken, grilled asparagus and baby potatoes. I avoid looking at my sister as we slip back into our seats, but I can feel her eyes drilling into me, taking in the fact that I disappeared with Shep. Well, she doesn't have to worry — nothing is going to happen between us. Unfortunately.

"So, Laurel told me that you're really into Greek mythology," Shep says, reaching for the potatoes.

I nod, surprised she'd mentioned that to him, of all things. Especially because she thinks my "obsession" with Greek mythology is super weird.

"I named my dog after Percy Jackson," he adds.

"I love that book!"

"Yeah? I've read the entire series a few times."

"You should read Lore Olympus," I say. "It's about Persephone and Hades."

"I'll definitely check it out." Our eyes lock and I feel that look all the way down to my toes.

I glance away first, a flush creeping into my cheeks. This isn't good. I can't let myself like Shep. Anything more than friendship has to be off-limits.

I'm distracted from my feelings when my mom drops a piece of chicken onto my plate. I glare at her. I hate it when she treats me like I'm two years old. How does she even know that I want chicken?

"So, Shephard," Mom says, handing the platter past me to him. "I hear you're going to York in the fall. What are you majoring in?"

"I'm undeclared." He slides some chicken onto his plate.

"I'm interested in a lot of different subjects. It's hard to decide which direction to go in, so I'm going to take a bunch of classes and see if I can narrow it down."

Mom smiles. "Well, I'm sure you'll figure it out." She turns back to Shep's uncle, seated on the other side of her.

I've barely eaten anything and the wine has hit me harder than I expected it would. By the time Shep finishes wolfing down his dinner, I'm feeling a little dizzy. He's reaching for a second helping of potatoes and I'm slopping more wine into my glass when the fiddler calls his name. He smiles encouragingly and holds his fiddle out towards him.

Shep shakes his head. "No, it's okay. I'm good."

"Come on, bro," Andrew says. The Tremblay's all start clapping and whistling. Shep swears under his breath, but the crowd just gets louder, not about to give up. Sighing, he stands up and walks over to the fiddler. He takes the violin and tucks it under his chin, then rests the bow against the strings. He closes his eyes and a moment later he starts to play.

Goosebumps break out on my arms as Shep carries us through the hauntingly beautiful melody, his fingers moving deftly on the strings, sawing the bow gently back and forth. His brow is furrowed, like he's lost in the music, transported somewhere far away from this orchard. Somewhere no one can reach him.

When he's done, he opens his eyes. There's a moment of silence and then everyone erupts into applause. My mom leaps up to give him a standing ovation, clapping louder than anyone else. From the way she's jumping up and down, I'm worried she's going to spill out of her lime green dress. Laurel catches my eye and makes a face. I smile and shake my head. We are always united on the subject of mom and how easily she embarrasses us.

Shep makes an exaggerated bow. He walks over and plunks back down beside me, grabbing another roll from the basket as the catering staff begin to clear the plates.

"That was amazing," I say.

"I usually stick to the guitar but they weren't going to let up until I went up there." His voice has an edge to it.

"You don't like to play?"

"What I don't like is being shown off like I'm some kind of party trick," he says. "My family loves to make a big deal about me when there's a crowd, but they don't really take me seriously as a musician."

"What do you mean?"

He shrugs. "I can count on one hand the number of times they've come to a school concert," he says. "And I busk downtown every weekend. They've never once come to watch me."

I picture him, guitar case laid open on the ground to collect bills and loose change, playing Hotel California or Blackbird like the musicians I've seen back home in Balboa Park.

I'm distracted by Andrew's friends laughter. They howl and slap him the back as the catering staff wheel out a huge cake in the shape of a brown recliner. One of his friends announces that it's a perfect replica of the chair they've bought the happy couple as a wedding gift.

Andrew beams. "Thanks, guys! That'll be perfect in our living room. I'll put it right in front of our new big screen TV."

Laurel's smile is frozen in place. Design is her thing and I know that inside she's silently screaming. An ugly brown recliner is definitely not on her Pottery Barn gift registry.

Andrew mimes throwing a football. "On that note, we're going to get the speeches started," he says. "Arden, you're up."

My stomach drops.

"From the heart," Shep reminds me.

But my heart is too busy pounding in my ears for me to even hear what it has to say.

I stand up, wobbling on my wedge heels, and look out at a sea of faces. Maybe it's my nerves, which have returned full-force, or maybe it's the alcohol, but everything is suddenly blurry.

Here we go...

I clear my throat. "Um, hi. I'm Arden. But I guess you already know that."

"Speak up," Mom says, poking me hard in the hip. "No one can hear you."

I glare at her. "I'm Arden," I repeat, a little bit louder this time. "Laurel is my sister. Obviously. She wanted me to give a speech, so...here I am." I laugh weakly.

It feels like there's something stuck in my throat, so I clear it again. "I'm really happy to be part of this wedding," I say. "Laurel is a great big sister. Really great." Everyone is staring at me, waiting for me to say something tender and touching, but all I can think about is the fact that I can't feel my legs.

"We haven't seen each other that much in the past few years, because, you know, she's been living here..." I swallow. "This is my first time in Canada. It's such a great country. Really beautiful. From what I've seen of it, anyway, which isn't much, mainly just the hotel, but I'm hoping to get out and explore the city bit."

Oh god, stop talking about Canada!

"Um. I'm sure Andrew and Laurel are going to be very happy together," I say, slurring slightly. My face is on fire. Maybe the wine wasn't such a great idea after all. I hope no one can tell that I'm drunk. "They're total opposites, but they say that opposites attract, right?"

Someone coughs.

"Anyway, Andrew's really great—" *stop saying great!* — "He likes fantasy football and travelling to Iceland and helping people with their mortgage needs. And you know, Laurel isn't into any of those things, but somehow they make it work. Because they're in love."

I'm rambling. I need to sit down before I make this any worse, but I'm like a runaway train. I can't stop myself. I seem to have no control over what's coming out of my mouth.

"I guess my point is that it's nice to know that people still believe in love, even when the odds are totally against them," I say. "Because, you know, the divorce rate is, like, fifty percent. Which is super, duper high. So, it's kind of crazy that anyone would decide to get married, knowing that it's probably bound to fail. I mean, I would never do it, but I guess it's good that Laurel and Andrew are willing to take the chance. They must really love each other."

I've managed not to look directly at anyone this entire excruciating time, but Dad and Rachel suddenly come into sharp focus. They're holding hands across the table. Dad shakes his head slightly — a warning — and something inside of me snaps.

"But, like, is love really enough?" I say. "You marry someone you're so sure you want to spend the rest of your life with, you have a beautiful wedding that costs an *insane* amount of money, you're supposed to be together forever, and somewhere along the way you just change your mind." I hiccup. "All those years together, all those memories, and where do you end up? Sitting on opposite sides of the table at your daughter's wedding because you can't get along for even one night. Totally embarrassing yourself and making everyone else uncomfortable."

Dead silence.

I sway on my feet.

"Marriage is *definitely* not for me. But I'm sure that Laurel and Andrew will be fine, whatever happens. And I'm sure that unlike *some* people if they did end up getting divorced they'd still find a way to be friends. They won't act like children, arguing over who gets to keep the ugly recliner." I start to laugh. "Don't worry, Andrew, Laurel isn't going to fight you for that chair."

No one laughs with me. I look at my sister and my stomach lurches. She's staring daggers at me, her face bright red.

Yikes, she's really mad.

I'd better wrap this up.

"Um, okay. That's it. Thanks," I mutter, feeling my own face burn. I sit down in my chair, wishing that I was invisible.

I *told* Laurel that it wasn't a good idea to make me give a speech.

"Well," Mrs. Tremblay says, smiling tightly at me. "That was...something. Thank you, Arden." I'm drowning in humiliation as she raises her glass and gives a lovely toast to the bride and groom, effortlessly saying everything that I should have said.

Underneath the table, Shep takes my hand. And he doesn't let go, not until long after I've stopped shaking.

MY HEAD HURTS.

My everything hurts.

I peel my eyes open. The room is as dark as night, thanks to the hotel's blackout shades, but the alarm clock on the nightstand informs me that it's already after nine am. I'm usually a pretty light sleeper so it's a testament to just how out of it I was that I didn't even hear my mom leave for her early morning workout at the hotel gym.

I need to get into the shower and grab some breakfast, make myself semi-presentable before the day's wedding activities begin. My sister has provided a typed agenda, very on-brand for Laurel, and a quick glance tells me that I'll be spending my day having lunch at a teahouse, followed by some light shopping downtown and capped off by the rehearsal dinner tonight.

But before I do any of that, I need to apologize to my sister.

I groan and slowly sit upright, my head pounding. I didn't get a chance to explain myself to Laurel last night —

right after my disastrous speech, my mom bundled me into our rental car and brought me back to the hotel. She didn't say much on the forty-five-minute ride from Andrew's parents' house into the city, but what was there to say, really? I could feel her disapproval coming off her in waves, so I knew it was bad — especially coming from my mother, who is usually the one doing all the embarrassing.

My face prickles just thinking about my speech, snatches of which come back to me now, making me want to bury myself under the covers and never come out. *The divorce rate is, like, fifty percent... you're supposed to be together forever... somewhere along the way you just change your mind... Andrew can keep the ugly recliner.*

Oh, god.

My speech went even worse than I ever could have imagined it would. I made a total fool of myself. And while I wish I could just lie back down and hide out from everyone — especially my sister — forever, I don't have a choice. This is Laurel's wedding weekend and it's supposed to be the best time of her life. I'm not going to ruin yet another moment for her.

I flick on the lamp and climb out of bed. I grab a bottle of water from the mini-bar and down it, along with some Advil I discover at the bottom of my mom's fake Fendi purse. My headache is not helped by my braid crown, which is pulling at my scalp and, after a night of sleep, now resembles a frizzy blonde halo. I'm still wearing my dress from last night, too — when I got back to the room, I collapsed into bed, too wrung out to even put on my pajamas.

I'm so anxious to talk to my sister that I don't even try to make myself look presentable. Secretly I'm hoping that if

Laurel sees how pathetic I look she'll take pity on me and let me off the hook. I pick up the key to her room from the desk. She gave me one of her extra room keys so I can act as her gopher. At the time I was annoyed, but now I'm glad to have the key so if she refuses to answer the door, I can just let myself into her room. Invasion of privacy? Yes. But I don't know what else to do. I have to make this right.

I head out of my room, wincing as I pull the bobby pins out of my hair. Laurel's suite is on the same floor but on the opposite end of the long hall. When I reach her door, I take a deep breath. My heart is pounding as I timidly knock. I'm not surprised when she doesn't answer. I knock again, louder this time, and then press my ear against the heavy wood. I don't hear any movement on the other side, so I slide the key card in and push open the door.

"Laurel?"

It's like walking into a cave — the lights are off and the blinds are closed. I can't see a thing. I've been in her suite several times already, so I know that it's an identical layout to my room, only bigger, with a king-sized bed set against the back wall where I assume my sister is still sleeping.

Great. Now she's going to be pissed that I'm waking her up. Then again, it's nine o'clock, so maybe she slept through her alarm.

"Are you awake?" I ask.

When she doesn't respond, I feel my way through the dark over to the nightstand. I flick on the lamp and frown.

The bed is empty. The sheets are rumpled, the white duvet cover pooled at the bottom of the bed.

Maybe she went for a run or went to visit one of the other girls in their rooms, I think, setting my fistful of bobby pins on her nightstand. I look around the room. Laurel is super organized, very a-place-for everything-and-everything-in-its place, so when I notice her suitcase is no longer on the luggage rack, I get a swoopy feeling in my stomach.

I check the bathroom. Her quilted Chanel makeup bag is no longer on the counter and neither is her hair straightener or her shockingly expensive hair products. My mouth is dry as I dash over to the closet. Her wedding dress — a gorgeous, off the shoulder ivory satin ballgown — is still hanging in the closet, her peacock blue heels neatly lined up on the floor.

I'm relieved that her wedding dress is still here. *Maybe she missed Andrew and decided to go home for the night.*

But then I spot an envelope with Andrew's name scrawled in blue pen resting on top of the desk and a pit starts to grow in my stomach. With a mounting sense of dread, I walk over and pick up the envelope. It isn't sealed and there's something lumpy near the bottom. I chew my lower lip, thinking. Something about the way his name is written bothers me. The penmanship is sloppy, like Laurel wrote it in a hurry, so different from her usual careful penmanship. I know I shouldn't open it, but I tell myself that if what's inside is just a love note to her soon-to-be husband, I will stuff it back into the envelope, mostly unread.

I unfold the note.

I'm sorry. I love you, but I can't do this.

My breath catches as I stare at the words, trying to make sense of them. I tip the envelope over, letting out a gasp as her engagement ring falls into my palm.

No.

No, no, no, no, no. This can't be happening! Laurel loves Andrew. Why would she do this? I may not know my sister as well as I once did, but I can't imagine she's changed so much in the past few years that she would do something as heinous as run out on her own wedding. She was fine yesterday. A little stressed, sure, but who isn't leading up to the biggest event in their lives? Overall, she seemed okay. Right up until...

My speech.

My heart drops. Wait. Did Laurel turn runaway bride because of what I said in my speech last night? Because what I said wasn't *that* bad. Was it? I mean, yeah, I shouldn't have mentioned divorce rates, I shouldn't have talked about our parents' terrible relationship, but was that really enough to make her ditch Andrew the day before their wedding?

Tears prick my eyes. Oh my god. I think this might be my fault. I think I've ruined my sister's wedding.

Okay, okay. Deep breath. I can fix this. I just need to call Laurel and smooth things over and everything will be fine. It will all be fine. I'll apologize and she'll come back and put her ring back on her finger and we'll destroy this note and pretend like none of this ever happened.

I don't know her number off-by-heart, so I can't call her until I get my cell phone from my room. I throw open the door, ready to run down the hall, but in my haste, I almost bowl over Shep, who's standing on the other side, his hand raised as if to knock.

"Arden," he says, smiling. "Good morning."

I blink. "What are you doing here?"

"Andrew wanted me to bring this present over for

Laurel," he says, holding up a small box wrapped in robin's egg blue paper and tied with a fancy white ribbon. "It's a wedding gift. He was too excited to wait until tomorrow to give it to her. I guess he thought she might want to wear it to the rehearsal dinner tonight."

My stomach lurches. Poor Andrew. He's blissfully unaware that he's been jilted and his fiancée has basically left him at the altar. If I can't convince Laurel to change her mind and come back, he's going to be heartbroken. I'm devastated for him and for my sister, who I know never would have taken off like this if she'd been thinking clearly. She never would have done this if I hadn't given that stupid speech.

Shep can obviously tell from the panicked expression on my face that something's wrong because he frowns. "Are you okay?"

I shake my head.

"What's the matter?"

I can't even get the words out, they're too awful, so I hand him the note and let him read for himself.

Shep's brow furrows. "Wait. She left?"

I hold up Laurel's engagement ring, a perfect square-cut solitaire on a thin gold band. My sister loves this ring. She was so excited when she called to tell us that Andrew had proposed and I know she hasn't taken it off once since he gave it to her. Not until I went and ruined everything.

"She's gone," I say, a lump forming in my throat. "And it's my fault. All that t-terrible stuff I said in my speech..."

"Come on," Shep says. "Your speech wasn't that bad."

But it was. Laurel never would have taken off if I hadn't said all those things. I know it.

"I need to call her," I say.

Shep digs in his pocket and pulls out his phone. He brings up Laurel's contact information and then hands his phone to me.

I try her, over and over and over again, but all I get is her voicemail. I send her a text, begging her to respond, even though I'm pretty sure that she's turned her phone off. She clearly doesn't want to be reached.

Shep rubs a hand across his face and sighs. "I guess I'd better call my brother and tell him what's going on."

I grab his arm. "No! Don't do that. I can fix this. I'm going to fix this. He doesn't have to know she's gone."

"Arden, the rehearsal dinner is in, like, eight hours," he says warily. "They're supposed to be getting married tomorrow. We can't keep this from him."

"I just need to find her so I can apologize," I say. Which is not going to be an easy thing to do, considering I don't know my way around this city. I don't even know how to get to her apartment from this hotel.

But Shep does.

"You have to help me find her," I say.

"I really think we should call Andrew—"

"Please," I say, tightening my grip on his arm. "I can't let this happen. I can't let her miss out on her wedding because I said something stupid."

Shep sighs and scrubs his hand through his dark blonde hair. "I just don't see how we're going to keep this a secret. She's the bride — people will notice that she's missing."

For a moment, I wonder if I should give up and just let him call Andrew. Maybe this is all for the best. Maybe Laurel realized that getting married is a crazy idea. Maybe I did her a favor, in the long run.

But I won't know whether that's true until I talk to her. And I won't be able to live with myself if I really am the reason that she cancelled her wedding.

"I'm going to find her before anyone notices," I say.

I hold my breath as Shep stares at me for a long moment. "Okay, fine," he says, giving in. "I'll help you look for her. But if we don't find Laurel in the next hour or so, then I'm going to have to—"

I don't let him finish. "Thank you!" I call over my shoulder as I run down the hall towards my room. "Just give me five minutes." I need to get out of this wrinkled dress and into something clean and grab my phone before he changes his mind.

four

WHILE SHEP REQUESTS an uber to pick to us up at The Hazleton, the beautiful boutique hotel where the wedding party is staying, I leave a message for my sister in her room, just in case she returns and for some reason has missed the eight hundred texts I've already sent her. I also shoot my mom and the other bridesmaids a message to cover for Laurel's absence. I tell them that she has a migraine and not to disturb her under any circumstances, which should buy me some time — at least until lunch rolls around and we're due to leave for the restaurant.

"I think we should start at their apartment," Shep says as we get into the elevator. "Andrew's golfing with my dad and the guys this morning, so he'll have left early. Laurel knows his schedule so maybe she's planning to stop by and get some of her stuff while he's out."

I shake my head. "But if she intended to go home, then why wouldn't she just leave the note for him at their apartment instead of in her hotel room?"

He shrugs. "Maybe she figured it would be less painful for him to find it at the hotel."

I nod. He's right — Laurel would have thought about that. For Andrew, discovering his fiancé has left him is going to be awful enough, but at least this way the memory won't be attached to their home. There's just one problem with that theory, though...

"But how did she expect him to find the note if it's at the hotel?" I ask.

"He's supposed to pick her up here later, before the rehearsal dinner. I guess she figured he'd see it then," he answers. His expression darkens. "You know, she really should have found the courage to break up with him in person. My brother deserves more than a note."

I want to defend Laurel, but really, what can I say? I can't argue that dumping someone via letter is terrible and cowardly. There really is no excuse for what she did, but I also know that the only reason she did it is because she's scared. It's not something I expect Shep to understand — his parents have been married for a hundred years, he has no idea what living through a divorce is like. All through my childhood, my parents fought so much that when they finally sat Laurel and I down and told us they were splitting up, I was relieved. That feeling didn't last long, though, because as it turned out being divorced didn't stop them from fighting — they just fought about different things. The arguments shifted from who took the garbage out last or forgot to buy milk to which one of them would get the Volkswagen or which holidays they'd get to spend with us.

"She's not breaking up with him," I say. "She's just confused."

"She wrote that she couldn't marry him and she gave him the ring back," Shep points out. "That doesn't sound like she's confused."

I look up at the numbers over the elevator door so I won't have to look at him. He's not wrong, returning the ring is a pretty solid statement, but I'm holding out hope that my sister chose to leave it at the hotel because she knew that Andrew wouldn't be coming by for hours — I bet she purposely built herself a window of time in case she changes her mind. And with any luck, she'll come to her senses and put her ring back on and Andrew will never need to know about any of this.

The elevator pings and the doors slide open.

"I know that Laurel loves your brother," I say to Shep as we head into the lobby.

He nods. "I know that, too. If I didn't, I wouldn't be trying to help you find her."

I give him a small smile. If there's anything to be grateful for, it's that Shep showed up when he did. I don't know what I would have done if I had to search for Laurel on my own in an unfamiliar city. I'd have no idea where to even look.

We walk past the front desk, out the glass doors and onto Yorkville Avenue. This section of the street is relatively quiet, lined with brown-stone buildings and leafy green trees, a marked difference to the skyscrapers rising into the sky just a few blocks away. We're right around the corner from the Royal Ontario museum — a weird-looking aluminum and glass building that I've been dying to check out — but sightseeing isn't on Laurel's tightly-timed agenda. I'd hoped to stick around for a few extra days and explore the city, but for some reason my mom has us booked on the first flight back to San Diego on Sunday.

The sun is already warm and the air is sticky, even at this early hour. I hope I don't sweat through my sundress.

"I still think we should start at their place," Shep says as the uber driver pulls up in front of the hotel in a blue Prius. "Even if Laurel isn't there, maybe we'll find a clue about where she might have gone."

I nod. Maybe he's right. And you never know, maybe Laurel will take advantage of the fact that Andrew is out to swing by their apartment and grab a few things.

Shep holds the back door of the car open for me and my stomach gives a little flip when he slides into the backseat beside me, his leg brushing against mine. I shouldn't be noticing how cute he is at a time like this, right? I mean, it's pretty hard *not* to notice — especially when he's exactly my type. And sitting this close, it's impossible not to smell him and he smells really, *really* good. Sort of citrusy, a scent I figure must be from his shampoo since his hair is still a little damp.

He has a faint shadow on his jaw, too, and his arms are tanned and have just the right amount of muscle and *oh my god, I have to stop this*. I should be concentrating on finding my sister and fixing this situation, not fantasizing about Shep! All my attention needs to be focused on the problem at hand, not on the boy beside me.

I just wish he didn't smell so good. It's very distracting.

While Shep gives Andrew and Laurel's address to the driver, I try my sister's cell phone again. And again I'm sent right to voicemail but I vow to keep calling her because at some point she'll have to turn her phone back on. When she does, I'll be able to track her through Friend Finder, provided she hasn't already anticipated this and turned her location off.

"So how come you're not going golfing with your brother?" I ask as the driver, an Asian girl with pink hair and a septum piercing, pulls away from the hotel.

"I hate golf," Shep replies. "It's so boring. Andrew didn't care if I ditched it because he knows I suck and I'd only hold them back. Other than asking me to deliver that gift to your sister, my time is my own until the rehearsal dinner tonight."

At the mention of the gift, I glance in my purse. The blue box is there, tucked beside the envelope with Laurel's engagement ring. Waiting for me to give them to her. My stomach tightens. I hope I get the chance.

Traffic is crawling. Shep and the driver chat while I stare out the window at the luxury shops on Bloor Street. Guilt washes over me. If I'd just done what Laurel had asked and actually written a speech like I was supposed to, instead of choosing to get drunk and trying to wing-it, then none of this would have happened. At this moment, we'd be eating strawberry French toast at the hotel restaurant, but instead I'm trying to figure out where my sister disappeared to, which feels next to impossible in a city of three million people. Especially when I only have a few hours to find her.

I send up a quick prayer: *Dear Lord, I swear, I won't complain about this wedding or anything else ever, ever again, just please let me find my sister. Please give me the chance to make this right.*

I'm suddenly feeling flushed. The hard truth is, I'm not going to be able to hold everyone off for very long — eventually someone (probably my mother) is going to ignore my instructions to leave Laurel alone with her "migraine" and they'll discover that she's missing. And then word will get out that she's gone and I will no longer be able to fix this and the world will end.

I close my eyes. If I thought that my sister was making the right decision by ending things with Andrew, if even a small piece of me believed that they weren't meant to be together, then maybe I could let myself off the hook about my awful speech. But I know how much she loves him. And I know, deep in my bones, that I scared her off of marrying him.

I've ruined my sister's wedding and probably her life and I'll never be able to make it up to her. Never. Once Laurel comes to her senses and realizes that all of this is my fault, she'll hate me. My parents aren't going to be happy with me, either — they've dropped an obscene amount on this wedding. Most of Laurel's guests have flown in from San Diego to be here for her big day, so I can only imagine how they'll react when they learn that they've wasted their money.

And Andrew. God. I can't bear to think about what cancelling the wedding will do to him. The humiliation he'll feel when he finds out that Laurel called everything off at the last minute.

"We're almost there," Shep says to me.

I open my eyes as the driver pulls up in front of Laurel and Andrew's red brick apartment building near Trinity-Bellwoods park. Laurel brought my mom and me to her place the other day, right after we landed, and I could hear the pride in her voice as she showed us around. The apartment is very Laurel — exposed brick walls, reclaimed wood floors, minimal furniture and decoration, no clutter. Like something out of a design magazine. My mom commented that it wouldn't be a great place to raise kids and my sister and I had rolled our eyes. Laurel might be getting married super young, but she's told everyone who will listen that kids aren't anywhere on the horizon just yet. And maybe not ever.

I thank the uber driver and Shep and I get out of her car and walk to the front door. Shep pulls out a key — it turns out that I'm not the only gopher this weekend — and we enter the lobby. The building only has four floors and while there is an elevator, we decide to take the stairs.

"What if she's not here?" I ask him. "Should we just hang around and see if she shows up?"

Shep frowns. "Maybe we should make a list of other places she might be. There's a coffee shop a few blocks away that I know she goes to a lot."

My chest tightens. I have nothing to add to the list because I have no idea where my sister spends her time. It's weird and wrong that Shep knows more about Laurel's life than I do, but I guess that's what distance has done to us. It's pulled us apart in ways that I never even anticipated.

Shep unlocks the door. Laurel and Andrew live on the third floor, in a spacious loft with floor-to-ceiling windows that let in a lot of natural light.

"Hello?" a voice calls.

Shep and I exchange a panicked glance. We just

assumed that Andrew would have already left for the golf course which, in retrospect, was kind of stupid.

"Hey, what are you guys doing here?" Andrew asks, wandering out of the bedroom, tucking his dark green golf shirt into his green-plaid shorts. He's wearing a white visor, his thick blond hair puffing over the top.

My cheeks burn. It's the first time I've seen him since my disastrous speech last night. Andrew's way too nice to ever confront me about why I thought talking about the odds of his marriage failing was a good idea, but I feel my words hanging awkwardly in the air between us. I owe him an apology, but I'm afraid that if I try to explain myself right now I'll slip up and tell him that my sister has left him.

I clear my throat. "Uh, we just stopped by to grab a few things for Laurel," I say. "I ran into Shep at the hotel and he offered to bring me to your place, since I don't know my way around the city. I think he was worried I'd get lost, ha ha."

My laughter sounds so hollow, so forced. I've never considered myself a good liar but Andrew seems to buy the story. Then again, why wouldn't he? He has no reason not to trust that I'm telling him the truth. In his wildest dreams, he'd never guess that we're really here to look for clues about where his fiancé might have run off to.

He smiles, the same friendly, easy grin as Shep's, and I send up another quick prayer that we'll find Laurel so that smile never leaves his face. "Did she like her present?" he asks me.

I somehow manage to grin back at him. "She loved it," I say, even though I can practically hear his perfectly wrapped gift beating like a tell-tale heart in my bag.

"I don't always pick up on her hints, but this one was pretty hard to miss, even for me," he says. "I'm glad I got it right."

I nod. Laurel is extremely hard to buy for, so I generally take the lazy way out and just send gift cards when her birthday or the holidays roll around. In return, my sister — who loves giving presents — always sends the perfect thing, something thoughtful and stylish that I usually love but never would have bought for myself.

"It's kind of strange," he said. "I haven't heard from her this morning."

I tense up.

"She's got a migraine," Shep says.

Andrew frowns, his eyebrows drawing together with concern. "Yikes, that's not good. I hope she's feeling alright in time for the rehearsal dinner. Migraines sometimes take her down for days."

I swallow. "I'm sure she'll rally. Don't worry."

But I can tell that his mind isn't at ease. My stomach tightens. Shep said that Andrew has a key to the hotel room — I really hope that he doesn't decide to check up on Laurel. He won't find my sister or the note she left him, but he will probably wonder why all her stuff is gone.

Andrew glances at his Apple watch. "Okay, well, I guess I'd better get going. Don't want to be late to tee off." He grabs his golf bag and slings it over his shoulder. "See you guys at the rehearsal dinner."

"Yeah," Shep says, patting him on the back. "See you there."

As soon as the door shuts behind his brother, Shep lets out a deep sigh and scrubs his hand over his face, while I clasp my hands together to try and stop them from shaking. Seeing Andrew in person and knowing that we're keeping this huge, life-altering secret from him has made this situation seem even more real.

"I feel sick," Shep says. He starts to pace. "I really don't know if keeping this from him is the right decision. What are we going to do if we don't find Laurel?"

"We don't have to worry about that because we're going to find her." I sound a lot more confident about this than I feel, but one of us has to remain positive or we'll both go to pieces. We're going to find Laurel because the alternative is too awful to think about.

I keep hoping that luck will be on our side and my sister will just walk through the door, but as the minutes tick by I'm more and more certain that she wouldn't want to return to their apartment so soon. It would be too painful for her. And there's nothing here that she truly needs — I know she has her laptop and some clothes, enough to get her by for a few days, anyway.

I glance around, looking for any clues about where she might have gone. I wander over to the scarred wooden table that Laurel uses for her desk. It's set against an exposed brick wall underneath a print of a mysteriously beautiful red-haired woman in a white nightgown. I know next to nothing about art, but I recognize this portrait because my sister sent me a link to a website that sold prints once, probably a hint for a gift that went totally over my head.

A large computer monitor and keyboard sit on the desktop, along with a brand-new sketchbook, a plain white coffee mug filled with expensive markers, and the evil eye bracelet she bought on our trip to Greece when I was twelve

— the last vacation we ever took together as a family. I'm surprised to see that she still has that bracelet. I lost mine ages ago.

There's also a glass fishbowl stuffed with stubs from what must be every concert or art event she's attended since she moved to Toronto. A soft pink cardigan hangs from the back of her rolling desk chair. I recognize that sweater — she bought me the same one in light blue for my birthday last year.

"Okay, let's make a list," I say, picking up the sketchbook and selecting a purple marker from the mug.

Shep sits down on the squashy grey couch and lets his head loll back against the pillows. "Let's see," he says. "We'll go to the coffee shop that I mentioned earlier first. It's not too far from here."

I write it down on the list.

"Okay. Where else?" I ask.

He shrugs. "I've heard her mention High Park — it's where Andrew proposed. And I think she sometimes goes to Queen Street. But it doesn't seem likely that she'd go shopping immediately after dumping my brother."

I can't imagine that she'd do that either, but I add Queen Street anyway, and then look expectantly at him.

"And...I'm out of suggestions," he says. "To be honest, I don't spend all that much time with her or Andrew. Especially lately, since they started going hard with the wedding planning."

I frown and tap the end of the marker against the sketchpad. The portrait above Laurel's desk catches my eye again — there's something about the red-haired woman, something about her watchful gaze that draws me in.

I pull out my phone and take a photo of her, then do an image search. "*The Marchesa Casati*. The original is hanging in the Art Gallery of Ontario," I say, looking over at Shep. "Maybe Laurel went there." Art is her favourite thing, her passion, and I can easily see her hiding out in a museum for hours, figuring that it was a safe place where no one would ever think to look for her.

"The AGO isn't too far from here, I guess we might as well check it out," he says, but he doesn't sound convinced.

My heart sinks. The truth is my sister could be anywhere. Toronto is a huge city and we don't have much time to try and find her — Laurel and I are supposed to meet the girls for lunch in a few hours.

"What if she isn't at any of these places?" I ask. While I think it's entirely possible that Laurel might have gone to a museum, it's also equally possible that she could be somewhere else — somewhere that would never occur to either of us to check. "She could be hiding out in another hotel or at a friend's house—"

My eyes widen. Friends.

"Wait," I say. "Her bridesmaids!"

Just because Laurel didn't tell me where she was going doesn't mean that she didn't tell *someone*. She might have let Charlotte or Nathalie or Riya know her plans. Or she might have taken them with her, for support. Maybe she's with them right now.

I can't believe I didn't think of this.

I set the sketchpad and marker down on Laurel's desk. Of the three girls, I'm friendliest with Riya, so I start with her. I stare at my phone, wondering what to say that won't set off alarm bells, just in case my sister isn't with her. I finally settle on:

Hey.

The three dots appear on the screen almost immediately, signalling that Riya is responding.

Hi! How is Laurel feeling? We're all so worried about her.

I chew my lip. Okay, so clearly the girls are still in the dark and Laurel didn't confide in them. On the one hand, it would be great if she was with them because mystery solved. On the other, it's better that she's not because the more people who know that she took off, the harder it will be to keep the news quiet.

Not good. Needs rest, I type.

Are you there with her? Your mom's about to come up, Riya replies.

I almost drop my phone. My mom! I knew that she wouldn't listen to me, that she'd completely ignore my instructions to leave Laurel alone. I wish that I could trust my mother with the truth, but I can't — she's not good in a crisis and she'd definitely send up a flare that Laurel is missing. She wouldn't be able to help herself.

"Everything okay?" Shep asks me.

I shake my head as I furiously type out a message to my mother.

Me: Do <u>not</u> come to L's room. She doesn't want to see anyone right now!!!!!!!!

I hold my breath, waiting for her response.

Mom: I told her all this stress would catch up with her! I'm just going to pop in for a minute. I have some peppermint oil. Maybe that will help.

Me: Mom no! She just fell asleep! She's going to be really mad if you wake her up!

Although my mom's more than happy to go nine rounds with my father, she generally tries to avoid fighting with Laurel and me. Pre-divorce, she never used to have a problem telling us off, so I think it's a more of a strategy to keep us from going over to the dark side, otherwise known as my dad and Rachel.

Mom: Alright, alright, I won't bother her.

I let out a breath.

A second later, another text:

Mom: Do you think she'll make it to lunch?

I smile. Not only did I somehow manage to talk her out of going to Laurel's room, but she's also just handed me a few more hours to look for my sister.

Me: No, but she still wants you guys to go. I'll stay behind to make sure she doesn't need anything.

Mom: There's no need for you to stay behind. You'll come to the tea.

It's an order not a request. Normally, I'd push back, but I don't want to push my luck. I'll figure out a way to get out of lunch.

And then, a moment later:

Mom: Why don't you come back to our room and let Laurel get some rest.

My heart starts to race. Crap. I can't let my mom know that I'm not in the hotel — despite the fact that she just agreed to leave Laurel alone, if she finds out that I'm not with my sister then she'll insist that I hang out with her.

Me: I'll come back when Laurel wakes up. I told her I'd stay with her.

I fill Shep in on the conversation, rip the list off the sketchpad and stuff it in my bag, along with my phone. "I don't think Laurel's going to come back here," I say. "We'd better start looking elsewhere."

He nods and stands up. "Agreed."

We're almost out the door, when I dash back in, grab Laurel's evil eye bracelet and slide it around my wrist.

five

SHEP nixes my suggestion that we request another uber to take us to the coffee shop, the first stop on our list of places to check for my sister. "The café is only a few blocks away from here," he says. "By the time the car arrives we could have already walked there."

"Yeah but it's, like, a thousand degrees out," I say. I'm used to hot weather — I grew up in San Diego where the only season we have is summer — but it's a different type of hot here. Uncomfortably humid, t-shirt-sticking-to-your-back-hot rather than the pleasantly dry warmth of my hometown. Riding in an air-conditioned car, even if we're only going a few blocks, seems perfectly reasonable to me.

"I thought Canada was supposed to be cold," I add, pulling my hair off my sweaty neck and into a ponytail.

Shep smiles and leads me from Laurel and Andrew's apartment building down a residential street crowded with narrow brick houses. "It's not usually quite this bad," he says. "I guess we have fossil fuels to thank for that." He shrugs. "Come back in January — you'll be buried up to your knees in snow."

"Honestly, that doesn't sound too bad right about now," I say. "I've never seen snow. It's not really a thing in southern California.

When we reach Trinity-Bellwoods park a few minutes later, Shep takes a shortcut, leading me down a rough cement path lined with leafy green trees. The park is full of joggers and people walking their dogs or sitting on wooden benches, families picnicking on the grass field. We pass a tennis court and a playground. Through the trees, I can see the CN Tower rising in the distance, by far the tallest building in the Toronto skyline — it reminds me of the Seattle space needle, only much bigger.

"Well, since you haven't seen snow, you'll definitely have to return in the winter," Shep says, picking up our conversation again. "I'll take you to the outdoor ice-skating trail in Etobicoke. And if you come near Christmas, we can go to the market in the Distillery district. We'll have glüh-wein and pretzels."

"What's glühwein?"

"It's basically red wine but with spices," he says.

I make a face, thinking of the red wine I guzzled last night at the welcome dinner and all the trouble it got me into.

"It tastes better than it sounds, trust me," Shep adds, stepping aside so a guy on a skateboard can pass by.

I smile and my heart lifts at the thought of coming back to Toronto to hang out with him again. And then I remember that what we're doing now isn't really hanging out — we're on a mission to find my sister — and the guilt settles back over me like a blanket. I need to be focused on righting my wrong, not planning my next trip to see Shep. Besides, if this wedding doesn't happen then it doesn't seem likely that we'll ever be drinking spicy wine or eating pretzels or doing anything else together, ever again.

I frown. If the situation were reversed and Andrew dumped Laurel the day before their wedding because of some dumb speech that Shep gave I would probably blame him, so it's hard to believe that if the worst happens and we don't find my sister that he would want to see me again.

I guess he can tell from the expression on my face that I'm starting to stress, because Shep reaches over and squeezes my arm. "Hey," he says. "Whatever happens, it's going to be okay, Arden."

I nod, but I don't really believe that's true. If Laurel doesn't go through with the wedding, all because of something stupid that I said, it will definitely not be okay.

We leave the park and walk a few blocks, passing by a bakery and a Vietnamese restaurant. Shep eventually stops in front of a brown brick building. He pulls open the door and we slip inside the coffee shop.

I shiver as a blast of air-conditioning washes over me. The café is bright and open and crowded with customers. A cool art installation is stretched across the ceiling, a grid that contains a bunch of bent white plexiglass pieces that look like paper airplanes. I can easily picture Laurel sitting on the blonde-wood bench built into the wall, hunched over her Mac or maybe reading one of the dog-eared mystery novels she loves so much.

Unfortunately, a quick scan of the room proves that she's not here.

My shoulders slump. *This is impossible*, I think. *We're never going to find her.* My sister may not be thinking clearly but she's not stupid. If she truly doesn't want to be found, then we won't be able to find her. She's probably holed up somewhere that she knows no one would ever think to check.

"Don't panic yet," Shep says. "We still have a few other places on our list."

I take a deep breath. I know that the odds are heavily stacked against us, but as long as there's a chance that we might find her — even if it's a very slim one — then we have to keep going. If we give up, then we'll have to tell Andrew that the wedding's off and I'll have to have to live with this mistake and I can't imagine doing either of those things.

"You're right," I say, reaching into my bag and pulling out the scrap of paper I tore from Laurel's sketchpad. "So, where should we go next?"

Shep runs his finger down the list, considering our options. "These places are kind of spread out all over the city, so we should tackle them in a way that makes the best use of our time," he says. "The AGO isn't too far from here, so let's go there now. If it turns out that Laurel's not there then we'll head to High Park. It's the furthest out, but we can hit the other places on the way back to the hotel. Sound good?"

My chest tightens at the thought of going back to the hotel without Laurel. I can't stand the thought of everyone I love finding out that I'm the worst maid of honor — the worst *sister* — in history.

"Sounds good," I agree, tucking the list back into my bag.

Shep gives me a sheepish look. "Would it be totally insensitive if I grabbed something to eat before we take off? I haven't had breakfast yet and I'm not going to be much good to you if my blood sugar takes a dive and I pass out from hunger."

I haven't eaten anything today either and the freshly-baked pastries behind the glass counter look amazing. Clearly this crisis hasn't affected my appetite.

I nod. "Okay, but let's get it to go."

While we wait in line, I take out my phone and try Laurel again, but I'm not surprised when I reach her voice-mail. I tap out another desperate text — *please, please, please call me back* — knowing even as I tap send that it's futile. But just in case my sister does decide to turn her phone back on, I turn the volume all the way up on my notifications so that I won't miss her.

Shep orders us each an iced coffee and a chocolate crois-sant, then tries to wave away my offer to pay, but I'm already holding a twenty out to the barista — it's my fault that we're in this mess, after all, and he's helping me. The least I can do is buy him breakfast.

"Thanks," Shep says to me as we grab our food and leave the café.

"No problem."

We walk back out into the blazing sun and I take a bite of my warmed-up croissant.

"Oh my god," I moan through a mouthful of flaky, buttery, gooey-chocolate pastry.

Shep smiles. "The best, right?"

"The best." I polish the rest of the croissant off in record time, then brush the crumbs from the front of my dress, slightly embarrassed that this incredibly hot boy just watched me inhale my breakfast without even coming up for air.

"You have some chocolate on your lip," Shep says, pointing at a spot near the corner of his mouth.

I blush. God, he must think I'm a total slob.

"How far away is the art gallery?" I ask, quickly wiping my mouth.

"Not too far," he says. "We just have to walk a few more blocks and then we can catch the bus. It'll spit us out right in front of the gallery."

I take a sip of my iced latte, relieved that we won't have to walk in this suffocating heat much longer. "By the way, what happened after I left the party last night?" My mom and I ducked out shortly after I gave that awful speech so I missed the rest of the evening.

Shep shrugs. "Not much. Everyone pretty much took off. Laurel wasn't in a great mood" — he looks over and gives me a sympathetic smile — "and she just wanted to go back to the hotel. The other girls went with her. Andrew and his buddies decided to go to some bar in the Fashion District. Your dad and Rachel stuck around for quite a while, though."

I grimace. That doesn't surprise me. Of course my dad jumped at the chance to be alone with Andrew's parents, to win them over without my mom hovering around, casting dirty looks in his direction.

Shep's eyebrows draw together in thought. "Hey, do you think that Laurel could be with your dad?"

I chew my lip. It hadn't even occurred to me that Laurel might run to my dad. She's barely speaking to him so I highly doubt that his shoulder would be the one she'd choose to cry on. Then again, my dad blew up his own life, so maybe he's exactly the person my sister would turn to right now. She knows that he wouldn't judge her. How could he?

"It doesn't hurt to check," I say, taking my phone out of my bag. I call my dad but it just rings and rings on his end before finally going to voicemail. I hang up without leaving a message, hoping that the reason he's not answering is because Laurel is with him and he's too busy comforting her to worry about answering his cell.

"Maybe we should just go see him," Shep says. "Where is he staying?"

I shrug. My dad and his wife aren't staying in the same hotel as the rest of the wedding party — my mom wouldn't allow it — and I was only half-listening when he told me which hotel he'd booked. "Somewhere downtown, I think."

"There are a million hotels downtown, so that doesn't help us much," he says with a sigh.

"Wait," I say. I open Friend Finder — I added my dad to my list months ago, although as far as I'm aware, he rarely uses the app. In a stroke of much-needed good luck, his avatar appears in the centre of a map of Toronto. I smile as I zoom in, bringing the surrounding streets into focus.

"Looks like he's at the Royal York," I say.

"That's right across from Union Station," Shep replies.

I debate sending my dad a message, but now that I think about it, if it turns out that Laurel is there with him it's probably better if we just surprise them. The last thing we need is for him to open his big mouth and tip her off — my sister would probably just take off again and go even deeper underground.

"Let's go," I say.

six

SHEP SUGGESTS TAKING the streetcar so I buy a transit pass at a nearby drugstore and then we walk to Queen Street. The streetcars and the buses look exactly the same to me — sleek and red and kind of futuristic-looking — but according to Shep they're not the same at all and the streetcar is an infinitely superior way to travel.

The tram pulls up a minute or so later in the centre lane — right in the middle of traffic, which seems like an accident waiting to happen. We have to dart across the street, dodging cars and a speeding cyclist to get on. Shep pushes a button on the door and it slides open. We hop on and he taps his fare card against the card reader. I follow his lead and tap my own card and then we squeeze our way down the crowded aisle.

Somehow we manage to find two seats together, which Shep claims is proof that miracles actually do exist. I slide into the window seat and he settles in beside me and for the second time this morning, I find myself sitting a breath away from him. I wonder if he's aware that our arms are touching — and if he is, whether his stomach is fluttering, too.

We've only just started to glide down the street, past restaurants and shops and several buildings covered in colorful murals, when my phone vibrates in my bag. I scramble to dig it out, praying that my sister is finally getting back to me, but when I see who's calling, my heart sinks.

I angle my phone so Shep can see MOM on the screen. We exchange a nervous glance.

"Maybe you shouldn't answer," he says.

"I have to," I reply. If I send my mother to voicemail, she'll just call back. Or, even worse, she'll charge down to Laurel's room, where she'll discover that neither of us are there. Obviously, I can't let that happen.

And so I take a deep breath and answer the phone.

"Hi Mom," I say.

"Hi honey. Is Laurel awake yet?"

"Nope, not yet."

"Okay, well, I was just talking to Bruno, the hotel concierge, and he told me that they have a doctor on call," she says. "He's arranged for her to come to the room and—"

"Mom, I already told you, Laurel just wants to be left alone!" I cry, shooting a panicked look at Shep.

"Honey, your sister will thank us when the doctor gives her something to take the edge off her migraine, believe me," she replies.

This is all perilously close to blowing up in my face. I close my eyes and pinch the bridge of my nose, trying to remain calm. When the doctor knocks on Laurel's door and no one answers, then word will get back to the concierge and the concierge will for sure tell my mother, who will for sure flip her lid. Oh god, why did I ever think that I'd get away with covering for my sister?

"The doctor should be there in about an hour," my mom says in her this-is-not-up-for-discussion-Arden-so-don't-bother-even-arguing-with-me voice. "But in the meantime, I need you to come back to our room and zip me up. And you need to start getting ready, too — we'll be leaving for lunch soon."

Right. High tea with my mom, Shep's mom and Laurel's bridesmaids. But as much as I love those little cucumber and cream cheese sandwiches, I don't have time for lunch. I need to spend every second looking for my sister.

"I feel kind of bad going to lunch without Laurel," I say. "I think it would be better if I just stayed with—" The rest of my sentence is drowned out by the sound of an ambulance speeding past.

"Arden?" my mom asks sharply. "Where are you?"

Crap.

"I'm just walking to the drugstore. I ran out to get a few things."

She tsks. "You should have told me. I would have come with you. I don't like the idea of you walking around an unfamiliar city by yourself."

"It's broad daylight." *And I'm not by myself.*

"Well, hurry back," she says. "And you're coming to lunch. You need to eat and Laurel will be fine on her own for a few hours. She's just sleeping anyway."

"Alright, alright." I guess I'm going to have to go with them to lunch — there doesn't seem to be any way around it. Not without raising my mom's suspicions, anyway.

"I'll see you shortly," she says, hanging up on me.

I close my eyes. This is a mess. My mom's expecting me to come to our room asap and she's not going to like it if I don't show up there soon.

"How far are we from my hotel?" I ask Shep, opening my eyes.

"Well, we're kind of heading in the opposite direction right now," he replies. "But if we jumped off the streetcar and took a cab we could be there in ten or fifteen minutes, depending on traffic."

Okay, so I could probably make it back to the hotel before my mom starts to wonder what's taking me so long. But rushing back means that I'll have to give up searching for Laurel, at least for now, and I just can't do that. Not yet.

"We're only ten minutes away from your dad's hotel, though," Shep adds.

That's all I need to hear. The lunch reservation isn't for another forty-five minutes —I'll just meet everyone there. With any luck, Laurel will be with my dad and I can beg her forgiveness and convince her to come to lunch and then no one will ever find out that she almost ran out on her wedding.

But first I need to get my mom out of my hair.

I send Riya a text, hoping that she'll be able to distract her. *Would you mind stopping by my room to help my mom zip her dress? And can you do me an even BIGGER favor and keep her busy until lunch? Just tell her that I'll meet you at the restaurant.*

Riya texts back a moment later. *Sure. Everything okay?*

It will be once I find my sister. And if I don't find her... well, then no, it definitely won't be okay. But as much as I like Riya, I can't tell her what's really going on, so I just send her a thumbs-up emoji.

"This is where we get off," Shep says. We stand up, swaying gently with the streetcar. He leans over and pushes the red stop-request button mounted on a steel pole. Through the window, I see a bunch of office buildings surrounding a plaza. In one corner of the plaza is a large reflecting pool with a row of recessed fountains spouting streams of water into the air. Just behind the fountains is the famous Toronto sign, seven huge, three-dimensional letters sandwiched between a maple leaf — Canada's national symbol — and a circle that's separated into four different colored sections.

"What does the circle represent?" I ask him as the streetcar rolls to a stop.

"It's a First Nations medicine wheel," he says. "The sign's actually a whole lot more impressive at night when you can see all the letters changing color."

The side doors whoosh open. We step out onto the pavement and I take a last look at the Toronto sign across the street before Shep starts to walk. It would be so great if I could spend the rest of the weekend just roaming the city, but once I find Laurel every second will be taken up with the wedding again. Which is how it should be. Still, I can't help wishing that I had some time to explore.

Instantly, I feel guilty — this weekend is supposed to be all about celebrating my sister and her fiancé, not about sightseeing. Or my burgeoning crush on a boy I just met, one that I probably shouldn't even be having feelings for in the first place.

I sneak a look at Shep and to my surprise I catch him

sneaking a look at me. I blush and crane my neck back, pretending to be fascinated by the buildings, which actually are pretty fascinating — they're so tall that I can barely see where they end and the sky begins.

"Pretty impressive, huh?" Shep says. "We're number three on the list of most skyscrapers in North America, after Chicago and New York."

"That is impressive."

He shakes his head. "God, listen to me. I sound like a tour guide," he says with a self-conscious laugh. "That's definitely not the impression I want to make on you."

My pulse races. *What impression does he want to make on me?* I think as a rush of feelings zip through me. There's another conversation going on between us, one that isn't about city signs or skyscrapers. It's in the way we're walking close together, our hands almost touching, the flush of our cheeks and the way our eyes skitter away from each other whenever they meet. Something is happening between us. Something that shouldn't be happening. Something that I don't think I can stop.

That maybe I don't want to stop.

We wait at the crosswalk for the light to change. Across the street, in front of Hudson's Bay department store, a man is playing a guitar, his case open in front of him. His reedy voice rises above the bumper-to-bumper traffic as he sings a slightly off-key version of Free Fallin'. It reminds me of Shep's amazing performance last night at the welcome dinner and what he told me about how he busks in the city on weekends.

"So, how come you're not going to study music?" I ask him. He's so talented and he plays like music is a part of him, but he told me that he's undeclared. It's hard for me to imagine why he'd waste his gift by doing anything else.

Shep shrugs. "According to my dad, music isn't going to take me anywhere," he says, digging in the front pocket of his khaki shorts. "And since he's the one paying for my tuition, it's not an option. He expects me to become a corporate drone, just like him and Andrew." His voice has an edge to it. The light changes and we cross the street. He tosses a few Loonies — the gold, Canadian one-dollar coin — into the man's guitar case as we walk past him.

"I get it," I say. "My dad's pushing me to go to Maryland, his alma mater. He's okay with me taking classical studies, but only because he thinks it's going to lead me to law school." I shake my head. "What he doesn't seem to understand is that I don't want to be a lawyer, but I guess I'll fight that battle once I finish my degree."

My dad put the same pressure on Laurel only my sister had the guts to stand up to him and forge her own path. I've always thought that was so brave, taking a leap and moving to a different country where she didn't know a single soul, all because she wanted a different life than the one that was being laid out for her. But now I'm wondering if that was Laurel's only motive — maybe my sister was running away back then too. Maybe this is actually how she deals with her feelings — by not dealing with them at all.

Up until I found her note this morning, I just assumed that my sister was happy — she's never once let on that she was having any doubts about marrying Andrew. I feel guilty for never asking how she was doing. Instead, I let her ramble on endlessly about bridesmaids dresses and seating arrangements when I should have been asking her the hard questions. Like whether or not getting married was something she really wanted to do.

Shep leads me down a set of concrete steps and I assume that we're taking the subway, but when we head through the glass doors at the bottom of the staircase we end up in a narrow corridor lit with fluorescent lighting and lined on either side with shops.

"This is the PATH," Shep says. "It's an acronym that doesn't actually stand for anything, believe it or not. It's just bunch of tunnels that run underneath the city. Super quick way to get around if you know the shortcuts, which I do, and a great way to get out of the heat in the summer and the snow in the winter. This route will spit us out right by your dad's hotel."

The PATH is basically one endless shopping mall. It's also a bit of a maze and I find myself quickly lost after we turn a couple of corners. There are mobs of people down here, most of them stylishly dressed, like they belong to this city. Tourists definitely stick out and I'm suddenly glad that I threw on a sundress and not my usual shorts and wrinkled t-shirt. I don't exactly fit in, but I don't stand out, either.

We go down a short flight of stairs, passing by a food court, a tailor, a nail salon. We walk by a newsstand and my eye is immediately drawn to the wedding magazines, photos of radiantly happy brides in frothy white dresses that I'm certain cost more than the average person makes in a month. It makes me wonder whether finding Laurel will really make a difference. My stomach tightens. Calling off the wedding might actually be the right decision for her.

If Laurel doesn't want to go through with the wedding then there's probably nothing that I can say to change her mind. Not that I want to change her mind — if that's how she feels, then she definitely shouldn't do it.

"Don't you think that Andrew and Laurel are too young to get married?" I ask Shep. "I mean, I can't imagine being ready to commit to someone for the rest of my life at twenty-one years old."

"Marriage is a big step, obviously, but they seem really in love," he replies. "I've always thought they were meant to be together. Soul mates."

I wish I had his optimism, but it's difficult to believe that love lasts forever when you've witnessed your family being torn apart by divorce. How do you ever know for sure that you've found the one? How can you trust that that person isn't going to change their mind someday?

We hang a right and walk down a narrow hall towards an escalator. As we rise into the grand lobby of the Fairmont Royal York, Shep glances over at me and gives me a smile that makes my heart catch and for the first time in my life I get why people take the risk. I'm still not sure that love is enough, but I'm starting to understand how you could be tempted to try and beat the odds.

seven

"I'M SORRY, I'm not able to give out guest information," the man behind the front desk says to me — Vishal, according to the shiny gold name tag attached to the lapel of his navy suit.

"But Kevin Stewart is my father," I reply. "And this is an emergency. I really need to talk to him."

"Perhaps you could give him a call?" Vishal looks pointedly at my cell phone resting on the counter.

"I *have* called him. Like a thousand times." My dad still isn't picking up and he hasn't returned any of my messages, which is not like him. I even tried Rachel's cell out of desperation, but she isn't answering either. It just makes me even more certain that Laurel must be with them and they're too busy consoling her to talk to me.

"Look, I know that he's here," I add, holding up my phone to show him my dad's avatar in Friend Finder. "See? He's the little blonde man in the blue golf shirt hovering right on top of this hotel. You can even see his name." It's printed in tiny letters above his tiny head.

When Vishal's expression doesn't change, I dig my wallet out of my bag and thrust my Westview High student ID card at him, tilting it away from Shep so that he can't see the worst, most unflattering picture of me ever taken. "Look — Arden Stewart." I tap my finger on the photo. "That's me. I'm Arden Stewart. Kevin Stewart's daughter."

Vishal gives me a sympathetic smile. "I wish that I could help you, Miss Stewart, but my hands are tied. I'm just not able to give out any guest information," he says. "It's hotel policy."

I sigh heavily and cram my ID back into my wallet. "Okay, fine. How about this? You call my dad's room and tell him that I'm down here waiting to talk to him. That's not breaking any rules, is it?"

Vishal shakes his head. "Like I said, we're not allowed to give out any guest information, so I can't confirm or deny that he's staying here," he repeats. "I wish I could help you but I can't."

"We get it," Shep says to him. "Thanks anyway."

"I don't understand what the big deal is," I mutter as Shep leads me away from the front desk. "I get that he can't tell us what room my dad's staying in, but the least he could do is call him for me."

"I guess it's a violation of privacy," Shep says. "They're probably worried they could be sued if it turned out you were a stalker or something."

"I'm not a stalker, I'm his daughter," I huff. "And I'm not going to give up." I didn't come all the way over here to not talk to my dad.

"I don't think we have an option," Shep replies. "No one's going to tell us anything."

Frustrated, I cross my arms and survey the lobby of the Royal York. This is by far the fanciest hotel I've ever been to, with its tile floors, ridiculously high warm wood ceiling and art-deco chandeliers. The lobby is two levels with a wrought-iron balcony that wraps around the length of the room, which is awash with golden light. The centrepiece is a huge gold clocktower with a built-in bar, shelves of back-lit liquor bottles on display. The bar isn't open yet, but I can easily picture groups of gorgeous, stylishly dressed people sitting on the black leather stools or lounging in the club chairs.

I try my dad's phone (again), growling when it goes through to voicemail (again). Seriously, even if he is with Laurel, he has to know that when someone calls you eight hundred times — especially when that someone is your daughter — that it's an emergency and therefore critically important to call them back.

"What do you want to do?" Shep asks me.

I shrug.

"Why don't we go back to our original plan and try somewhere else on our list?" he suggests. "We can't waste time wandering around the hotel hoping that we'll just bump into your dad. Laurel might not even be with him."

My shoulders slump. He's right. I know he's right, but it kills me to have to give up when there could be a chance that my sister is here. But I have to meet my mom and the others all the way across town for lunch in less than thirty minutes and if I don't show up at the restaurant my mother will freak and this house of cards will come tumbling down.

As we start to walk towards the black marble stairs that

will lead us down to the revolving glass door at the front entrance, I notice another set of three steps just off to the left. There's a small sign attached to a marble column marking the entrance to Library Bar. My skin prickles. If there's one place in this hotel, other than his room, where I might find my dad, it will be in that bar.

"Where are you going?" Shep calls after me as I veer off course. I head up the steps and through the door into a cozy, burgundy-walled room with thick carpet and heavy swag curtains covering the windows. The bar is made almost entirely of dark wood — the tables, the trim, even the panels on the ceiling — and it's totally empty, aside from one person sitting in a brown velvet wing chair, a cut-glass tumbler with a swirl of amber liquid set on the table in front of him.

My dad.

A rush of relief goes through me, followed by an even bigger rush of disappointment. He's alone. Laurel isn't with him.

My dad picks up his glass, about to take a drink, when he spots me barrelling towards him. "Ardie," he says, giving me a shocked smile. His face is drawn and pale, his thinning blonde hair standing on end as if he's been running his fingers through it. "This is a surprise. What are you doing here?"

I hesitate. Believe it or not, I really didn't think this over. I was so sure that Laurel would be with him that I didn't plan what I would say to him if she wasn't here. I'm at a loss about how to explain why I came all the way across the city to see him. I'm afraid that if I tell my dad that Laurel's missing then he'll send up a flare and all hell will break loose and I'll never have the chance to fix my mistake.

Think, brain, think!

But my brain refuses to cooperate. My brain is totally letting me down.

And so I stare at my dad in panicked silence for a long moment before he sighs heavily and says, "I assume you're looking for your sister."

I let out a breath of relief. "She's here?"

He shakes his head. "She *was* here. She showed up with her suitcase just as Rachel and I were getting ready to do some sightseeing."

My legs suddenly feel weak, so I drop down in the wing-back chair across from him. "What did she say?"

He grimaces and takes a swig of his drink. "She said she isn't sure that she wants to get married after all. She's having second thoughts, but I guess you must already know that if you're here looking for her."

Tears sting my eyes as I tell him about finding her note this morning, her engagement ring stuffed in the envelope. "I called you a thousand times," I say, glaring at him. "Why didn't you answer?"

His brow furrows. He turns over his phone, which is lying face-down on the table, and glances at the screen. "Oh, I guess I forgot to turn the ringer back on. I put my phone on silent after Laurel left. I wasn't ready to deal with the after-math," he says. "But back up a second — are you saying that Andrew doesn't know that the wedding's off?" His furry eyebrows rise up his forehead. "I just assumed Laurel told him in person."

I shake my head. "She didn't. And no one else knows that she's missing."

"What? You haven't told your mother?"

I shake my head and fill him in about Laurel's 'migraine.'

"She's going to find out sooner or later, Ardie," he says.

"Maybe not," I reply. "I just need to find Laurel. I have to make sure that she's cancelling the wedding for the right reasons." *And not because of my awful speech.*

My dad frowns. "Toronto is a huge city, Ardie. She could be anywhere."

"We have a list of places to check."

"Who's we?"

"Oh, Shep — Andrew's brother — is helping me look for her."

I turn around and look over my shoulder, but Shep obviously didn't follow me into the restaurant. He must have chosen to wait outside to give my dad and me some privacy. My heart starts to pound. I really hope that he's still here and he hasn't left to go talk to Andrew.

"So Shep knows about Laurel, too?" my dad asks.

I turn back to my dad. "Yes, but like I said, he's trying to help me find her so I can fix this."

"Fix it? I'm not sure that's possible, honey," he says. "I think it's pretty clear that your sister has already made up her mind."

My lower lip starts to tremble. "I have to try, Dad," I say. "That horrible speech I gave last night scared her off. I know it." I sniffle. "What if I've ruined her life? She'll never f-forgive me!"

"Ardie, you didn't ruin her life," my dad says, reaching across the table and patting my arm. "Your sister is an adult, fully capable of making her own decisions. So your speech wasn't so great...so what? I really don't think that's the reason she's decided not to get married."

"It certainly didn't help."

"Well, I know that you didn't set out to deliberately hurt her," he says. "I'm sure Laurel isn't mad at you. And...if it makes you feel any better, you're not the only one who said something you shouldn't have to her last night."

I take a shuddering breath and pick up the cloth napkin on the table, dabbing at my eyes. "What do you mean?"

He scratches his forehead, shifts in his seat. "I might have asked her whether she really wanted to go through with the wedding. I told her that if she had any doubts at all then she shouldn't get married."

"Dad!"

He winces. "I know, I know. I shouldn't have interfered," he says, holding up his hands. "But she didn't seem that happy to me. I wanted to make sure that she knew what she was getting into and that she was really ready for this. Anyway, she got very upset with me." He closes his eyes for a moment and when he opens them again, I can see that they're glassy with tears. "Andrew is a very nice guy, he seems to treat her well and I'm sure that she loves him, but if Laurel's not one hundred percent sure about marrying him then she definitely shouldn't do it. For both their sakes."

I can't exactly argue his point — I'd had the same thought earlier — but I'm still worried that my sister isn't thinking clearly to make the right decision.

"I've seen too many people get married when their hearts weren't really in it simply because they don't want to disappoint anyone," my dad says. "And let me tell you it's a hell of a mess to unravel once they realize they've made a mistake and they don't really want to be married. As painful as it is, calling the wedding off at the last minute is better for Laurel and Andrew in the long run."

"But what if she just has cold feet?" It's entirely possible that my sister is just running scared, reeling from the one-two punch of my awful speech and my dad's unsolicited — and very biased — fatherly advice. Of course he would tell Laurel not to go through with the wedding — I mean, not only is he a divorce attorney, but he got married young too and we all know how well that turned out.

"In my experience cold feet are a pretty clear sign," he says. "It's a big neon billboard telling her not to go through with it."

"I still need to talk to her," I say. "Do you have any idea where she might have gone?"

My dad shakes his head. "All she told me is that she needed time to think," he replies. "I offered to get her a room here but she didn't want to stay. She asked me to hold on to her suitcase for her but she didn't say when she planned to come back for it."

I feel a faint glimmer of hope. If Laurel told him that she needs time to think then that has to mean she isn't sure about calling off the wedding. Which makes me more deter-mined than ever to find her. I can't let my sister make such a huge, life-altering decision if she's not one hundred percent sure that she's making the right one.

Of course, I still have no clue where in this city Laurel might be, so that's definitely still a problem.

I chew my lower lip. "Have you told anyone that she's thinking about calling the wedding off?"

"Just Rachel," my dad replies. "To be honest, she's mad at me for what I said to Laurel last night. She thinks that your sister never would have thought about breaking things off with Andrew if I hadn't said anything." He sighs heavily and runs a hand over his face. "I don't know. Maybe she's right." He taps his fingers against his glass then drains the rest of his drink.

So that's why he's down here, drowning his sorrows in scotch — his wife is angry with him. I suddenly feel guilty that I haven't put much effort into getting to know Rachel. My dad may have moved on faster than Laurel and I would have liked him to but blaming his new wife for that isn't fair. Really, the most important thing is that he's happy — and that he found the courage to take another chance on love after what he went through with my mother.

I stand up. "I'd better get going," I say. "Call me if you hear from Laurel."

"I will."

I rush out of the bar and I'm relieved to see Shep leaning against the wall, scrolling through his phone.

"Hey," I say. "So it turns out that Laurel was here but she took off and she didn't tell my dad where she was going. We just missed her."

Shep sighs. "Great."

"I still think that she might be at one of the other places on our list," I say, as we start to walk quickly towards the hotel doors. I am running waaaaay behind now, I'm going to be super late for lunch with my mom and the girls, but there's nothing I can do about that. I'll just have to come up with a believable excuse on my way to the restaurant.

"I've been thinking it over," Shep says as we jog down the stairs, through the doors and past the doorman, a tall guy in a flat black cap and long burgundy coat with gold buttons. "Keeping all of this a secret from my brother just doesn't feel right to me. We really need to tell him what's going on."

I grab his arm and give it a little shake. "No! We can't do that yet," I say, my voice rising. "We still have a few more hours until the rehearsal dinner. I'm sure that we're going to find her." I'm not sure of this at all, but I'm not ready to give up yet.

"I just think that the longer we put this off the harder it's going to be to tell him," Shep says. "And then when we do tell him, Andrew's going to be really mad that we didn't come to him as soon as we found the note. I know my brother."

"He's not going to find out," I say. "We're going to find Laurel and then he'll never have to know about what happened today." Of course I have no way of guaranteeing that — my sister might still decide to call off the wedding. But even if she sticks by her decision, the least I can do is find her and insist that she have the guts to deliver that news to Andrew herself. I can't let him learn that he's been ditched through a note.

"You promised you'd help me," I add.

Shep sighs again.

"You said they're meant to be together."

He glances away from me and I know I'm getting through to him.

"Please," I say, folding my hands under my chin and staring at him from under my lashes. "Please please please please—"

"Alright, alright," he says, laughing a little. "You win. But if we don't find Laurel at any of the places on our list within the next few hours, then we're telling Andrew. Deal?"

If we don't find her at any of those places, then we'll have no choice.

I smile at him. "Deal."

eight

TWENTY-FIVE MINUTES LATER, the cab pulls over at the corner of Bay and Bloor and Shep and I get out. The mid-day traffic is horrible but Shep insisted that a taxi was still the fastest way to get to midtown — it wasn't fast enough, though, because I am so, so late for lunch.

"I'll meet you back here in an hour," he says.

I nod and pass him Laurel's hotel room key. While I'm drinking earl grey and eating scones with clotted cream and raspberry jam, he's going to hang out in Laurel's room so that he can intercept the doctor the concierge called to treat my sister. Because if the doctor shows up and no one answers the door then she'll probably complain to the hotel, who will then complain to my mother, and that would not be good. I briefly considered pretending to be Laurel and calling to cancel the appointment myself, but unfortunately my mom didn't tell me the doctor's name and I was too nervous to deal with the concierge.

Shep gives me an encouraging smile before turning and walking down the street towards the Hazleton. My chest tightens as I watch him go. I'm nervous that he'll break his promise to me and tell Andrew that Laurel has ditched him — I mean, I'm not sure that's a secret I could keep if the situation were reversed, especially because my loyalty is to my sister — but I guess I'll just have to trust him.

My heart starts beating a little faster as I head in the opposite direction, dodging people and the millions of pigeons that seem to be everywhere. I'm not ready to face my mother, but it's not like I can put this off any longer. I texted her on the ride over to let her know that I was on the way, but she hasn't responded, which means that she's mad at me. I still have no idea how I'm going to explain why I'm so late. Fortunately, we'll be surrounded by Laurel's friends and other diners in the restaurant, so maybe that will prevent her from making a scene — although that's certainly never stopped her before.

I walk over a subway grate and a blast of hot air causes the hem of my navy cotton sundress to flutter. This part of the city is mostly made up of skyscrapers, the ground floor space taken up by upscale chain stores and fancy restaurants. Bikers whiz past me in the green-painted lane that runs alongside the street, moving much faster than the traffic, which is almost at a standstill.

The teahouse is two blocks away from where we asked the cab to drop us off. I peek through the window and my chest tightens. My sundress, beaten-up navy converse sneakers and frizzy ponytail are way too casual for this place but there was no time to go back to my hotel and change so I'm just going to have to make it work.

I take a deep breath and pull open the door. The restaurant is whimsical, very Alice in Wonderland, with buttery yellow walls, grass green trim and red and white checkerboard floors. It's also packed with people but I quickly spot Riya, Nathalie, Charlotte, Mrs. Tremblay and my mother sitting around a long, colorfully set table at the back of the room, silver tiered platters of crustless sandwiches and tiny desserts in front of them. It's impossible to miss them — they're all wearing matching hot pink frisbee-looking hats covered in black feathers, the kind of thing that Kate Middleton might wear to a wedding.

My heart is pounding hard as I approach the table, avoiding looking directly at my mother. I can feel her tracking me, staring stonily over the rim of a rose patterned teacup.

"Hi Arden," Riya says cheerily.

"Hi," I say. My face feels like it's going to burst into flames as they all stare at me, waiting for me to explain why I'm so inexcusably late to my own sister's bridal lunch. Of course, Laurel isn't here but they've excused her because she's not feeling well — me, not so much. I mean, I do have a very good reason for not being here on time, I just can't tell them what it is.

After an uncomfortable moment of silence, Riya says, "I saved you a seat," and gestures to the wrought-iron chair beside her which, lucky for me, is the furthest point away from my mom. I sit down, relief coursing through me. Riya didn't just save me a seat, she saved me from a lecture — at least for the moment.

Nathalie is across the table from me, and she passes me a hat — only she calls it a "fascinator" — the same black-feathered frisbee they're all wearing. The fascinator is attached to a headband, and I slide it over my hair, smiling shakily as Charlotte holds up her phone and snaps a photo.

"I'm trying to capture every moment, so Laurel doesn't feel like she missed anything," she explains, taking another picture as I reach over and lift a cucumber and cream cheese sandwich off the bottom tier.

Taking photos for Laurel is a super thoughtful gesture, but it also makes me feel even worse about this whole situation. My sister planned this lunch to thank her bridesmaids for being part of her wedding and I worry that these photos will just serve as a reminder of everything that she missed out on, all because of me. And my dad, too, I guess. These are memories that she's never going to have now.

I stare miserably at my sandwich. I'm not even hungry, but my mom will notice if I don't eat and she'll grill me about it. Also, if my mouth is full then I don't have to talk.

"How is Laurel feeling?" Mrs. Tremblay asks me as I take a bite of the sandwich. "We've all been so worried about her."

So much for not having to talk. I chew slowly, trying to keep the panic I'm feeling off my face. It's so much harder to lie directly to Shep's mother — to any of them, actually. After a minute, I swallow and say, "A little better," but then I realize that my mom will probably take that as permission to check up on Laurel as soon as she gets back to the hotel, so I hastily add, "I mean, she's still in a lot of pain. She told me to thank everyone for their concern, but to please leave her alone, she needs her rest."

Mrs. Tremblay frowns and fiddles with one of her pearl earrings, which is when I realize that I might have come across as a little rude. I don't want her to think badly of her future daughter-in-law — especially because I totally made Laurel's response up — and I don't want her to think badly of me, either. I just want to keep everyone away from my sister's room so they don't discover she's missing.

"I'm paraphrasing, of course," I add hastily, praying that Shep's mom doesn't hate me now. I'm sure she already thinks I'm a little unhinged, after the speech I gave last night.

"Do you think Laurel's going to make it to the rehearsal dinner?" Nathalie asks me, her brown eyes widening. Her hair cascades in dark waves over her shoulders. She's wearing a sheer white blouse and I can hear my sister's voice in my head complaining about her friend daring to wear white when she isn't the bride. It almost makes me smile.

"She'll be there," my mom says firmly. "She's going to feel much better once she's given something for her migraine." She glances at the gold watch on her wrist. "In fact, the doctor should be arriving at her room any minute now."

I look down at my lap, my stomach churning. I really hope that the doctor isn't mad when she learns that we wasted her time. Shep's reassured me that won't happen because her office will still charge us for the visit, regardless of whether or not there's a patient to examine. I gave him most of my vacation money so he could pay the bill on the spot. I just hope it's enough to cover the full amount.

I'm mostly silent as we continue to eat, listening to Riya, Nathalie and Charlotte as they reminisce about their days at Ontario College of Art and Design while my mom and Mrs. Tremblay have a whispered conversation at the other end of the table. I can't imagine what they're talking about — they couldn't have less in common, but they seem to be getting along pretty well.

"So Arden, what was up with that speech you gave last night?" Nathalie asks, drawing me into the conversation.

"Nat." Charlotte shakes her head.

"What?" Nathalie says, shrugging. "Let's be real — we're all wondering what possessed her to give that speech. It was really out there."

My cheeks burn and I sink a little lower in my seat. "I didn't plan to say any of that. It just sort of came out," I reply. "And I'm not great at public speaking." Or at holding my alcohol, apparently.

Riya rolls her eyes. "Arden don't listen to her. Your speech wasn't that bad."

"Public speaking is, like, the number one fear," Charlotte adds. "Even above death."

Nathalie snorts. "You'd rather be dead than give a speech? That makes no sense."

I don't know. I sort of understand it.

I appreciate Charlotte and Riya coming to my defense. Of course, they probably wouldn't be defending me if they knew that what I said actually convinced Laurel to cancel her wedding.

"Thank god she didn't ask me to give a speech," Charlotte adds. "I hate being the center of attention. I'm already breaking out in hives thinking of standing up at the altar tomorrow."

Well, lucky for her, she might not have to worry about that.

Nathalie picks up a pair of tiny silver tongs and tosses a

lump of sugar into her tea. "Speaking of being the center of attention...remember that time we went to the Shameful Tiki Room," she says, starting to laugh.

Riya shakes her head, but she's smiling. "Nat, don't. Laurel would *kill* us for sharing that story."

"Oh come on, it was hilarious," Nathalie replies.

"I can't believe that she didn't realize that guy was standing right behind her the whole time," Charlotte says and the three of them dissolve into uncontrollable giggles. I grab a purple macaron from the top tier of the tray, feeling super uncomfortable and out of place. I suppose I should be grateful that they're not focused on me any longer, but their inside jokes and trips down memory lane are making me feel like even more of an outsider. It's also a painful reminder that they're closer to my sister than I am, that they know things about her that I don't know and maybe never will. The gulf between Laurel and me has never felt so wide and insurmountable as it does at this moment.

As I chew my macaron — blackberry, seriously amazing, why can't everything taste as good as this? — it occurs to me that maybe I can use the girls' closeness to Laurel to my advantage. I'll just gently press them for information that might lead me to her.

"You guys were all roommates in university, right?" I ask them. "You lived with Laurel?"

"Charlotte and I did," Riya says. "But Nat chose her boyfriend over us."

"*Ex*-boyfriend," Nathalie says, tucking a strand of her dark hair behind her ear. "And ugh, please don't remind me. Worst choice ever. Remind me what I even saw in him?"

Riya shakes her head. "Beats me."

"He was pretty cute," Charlotte says. "And he was in a band. What was it called again?"

"Bad Rubbish."

They laugh.

"Where was your apartment?" I blurt before they start remember when-ing again. I know that I'm grasping at straws, but it's possible that my sister might have been drawn to the comfort of her old stomping grounds. I do recall her telling me once about how much she loved rooming with the girls and how sad she was to leave them behind when she moved in with Andrew, but I have no idea which area of the city they lived in.

"Dufferin Grove," Charlotte says. "We had the main floor of this gorgeous old redbrick Victorian house. There was only two bedrooms and since there were three of us we had to draw straws to see who would share — Laurel won, so Riya and I ended up in the same room, but the rent was super cheap so it was totally worth it."

Dufferin Grove. I make a mental note to tell Shep we need to add that neighborhood to our list of places to check for my sister.

"I loved that house, even if it was haunted," Riya says, slathering a thick layer of apricot jam on her scone. "And I really miss living with you girls."

"I miss it, too," Charlotte says. "Sharing an apartment with Pete isn't nearly as fun. Although it does come with other benefits." She smiles suggestively.

"Wait, your house was haunted?" I ask. Laurel never mentioned anything about that, but I guess I shouldn't be too surprised — she told me barely anything about her life here.

Riya nods. "Nothing too scary, just, like, lights flickering and doors slamming shut, that type of thing." She looks over at Nathalie. "Hey, remember that place we used to go for brunch every Sunday? Forsythe's?" Before either of them can answer her, she says, "It closed down a few months ago."

"Aw, boo." Nathalie frowns. "They had the best waffles. And their mimosas were to die."

"So, do you see Laurel a lot?" I ask them, hoping to steer us to places they've all been together, but Riya just shrugs.

"She's been pretty busy over the past year with work and the wedding," she says. "And, you know, things change when you're in a relationship. She spends most of her free time with Andrew now. But I mean, we're all busy, too, it's not just on her. Life tends to get in the way sometimes."

The conversation segues away from Laurel to their own too-busy lives and I'm not sure how to bring it back around to the old days again, when the four of them used to hang out all the time.

No one seems in a rush to finish lunch and I'm wasting time sitting here, listening to them complain about their jobs and their significant others (or lack thereof), when I should be out looking for my sister. I begin to feel antsy — my hour is almost up and I'm sure that Shep's already at the corner, waiting for me, but it's not like I can just get up and leave. Not without everyone wondering where I'm going. I debate whether I should risk my mom's wrath by sending him a quick text — she has an ironclad rule about phones at the table — but decide against it. She's already mad enough at me as it is.

Finally the last mini cream puff has been eaten and the waitress arrives to clear the silver trays. I'm expecting her to go get the bill but instead she brings out a tray of champagne.

I sigh inwardly and shift in my chair. This lunch is never going to end.

Five minutes later, my cheeks are starting to hurt from smiling and my arm is growing tired as we continue to hold our flutes in the air, waiting for the waitress to snap another photo — Charlotte has made her take at least a thousand of them, just in case one of us blinks or makes a weird face.

"To Laurel," Riya says. "The best friend, sister and daughter that any of us could ever ask for. I know that my life is richer for knowing her. I'm so thankful that she and Andrew have found each other and I know that they're going to have a lifetime of love and happiness together."

See, this is why Riya should have given the speech last night.

My smile wobbles. The guilt feels almost overwhelming and it takes everything in me not to burst into noisy tears. Laurel should be here for this. This should be the happiest time of my sister's life — instead she's hiding out some-where, distraught and heartbroken, while we celebrate without her. All because of some dumb thing I said.

"To Laurel and Andrew," they all chorus and we clink glasses.

I take a small sip of champagne. It doesn't taste too bad — it's much better than the wine I had last night — but the bubbles tickle my nose, making me feel like I need to sneeze. I'm not looking for a repeat of what happened last night when I got drunk, so I pass my almost-full glass to Nathalie and stand up and excuse myself so I can go and text Shep.

I head to the washroom. I lock myself in a stall and send

him message to let him know that I'm running behind but I'll be there as soon as humanly possible, and then I try Laurel's cell again.

According to my English teacher, Mr. Leung, Albert Einstein once said that the definition of insanity is doing the same thing over and over again but expecting different results. Well, clearly I am insane because I keep hoping that if I call my sister just one more time then she'll finally answer. But of course she doesn't. And her mailbox is now full.

When I hear the bathroom door open, I slide my phone back in my bag, flush the toilet and leave the stall. Riya is standing at the sink, reapplying her lipstick. Our eyes meet in the mirror as I walk over to the sink next to her and turn on the tap.

"So, what are you doing after lunch?" she asks. "The girls and I are going to hang out by the pool, get some sun — you want to come with?"

My stomach drops. According to Laurel's schedule, we've been blessed with a few free hours until we're due at the rehearsal dinner tonight. I've been so busy worrying about trying to find my sister that I didn't think about what the others would be doing this afternoon. I also didn't think about how I'm going to extricate myself from the group after lunch. At the very least, they're going to expect me to go back to the hotel with them — unless I can find a good excuse to ditch them.

"Thanks, but I think I might explore the city a little bit," I say. "Shep's offered to show me around."

As soon as the words are out of my mouth, I know it's exactly the wrong thing to say. If Riya mentions my plan to my mom, she'll flip her wig. There's no way she'd be on board with me spending the afternoon 'running around the city' with a boy, even if he is Andrew's brother.

Riya smiles and nudges me in the side with her elbow. "Arden, you sly dog," she says. "Shep's a great guy. Good for you."

Every drop of blood in my body rushes to my cheeks. "It's not like that," I say. I mean, I kind of wish it was like that, but it's not. While I can't deny that I'm attracted to Shep and I'm sure that hooking up with him would be fun, I can't let my hormones make decisions for me. Besides, I have more important priorities right now.

"Too bad," Riya says, but I can tell that she doesn't really believe that I'm not into him. Of course, it would help if I wasn't blushing so hard. Gah, all my feelings show up on my face.

"We're just friends, but the thing is, my mom isn't going to be thrilled that I'm hanging out with him." Understatement. "She'll be expecting me to spend time with her."

"Well, maybe I can help you with that," Riya says.

Maybe she can.

I could just tell her that Shep and I want some time alone — it's clear that she'd cover for me — but I find myself wanting to let her in on what's really going on. She's one of Laurel's best friends, my sister trusts her and so maybe I should too. And she might be able to help me track her down.

I swallow, hoping I'm making the right decision and I'm not about to make everything worse. "Riya? You can't breathe a word of what I'm about to tell you," I say. "Not to anyone. Promise?"

The tone of my voice causes her smile to fade and worry to fill her eyes. She reaches out and rests her hand on my arm. "I promise."

I stare at the red and white tiled floor for a moment, my heart racing. "Laurel hasn't got a migraine," I say. "She's not sick. She's not even at the hotel."

Riya blinks. "What do you mean? Where is she?"

"I don't know," I say, a lump forming in my throat. As I tell her about the note, Riya's eyes get wider and wider.

"Oh my god," she says, her hand coming to her mouth. "I don't understand. Why would she do that?"

My stomach tightens. "I think she just panicked," I say. "I scared her with my stupid speech and then my dad said something to her that he shouldn't have. It freaked her out." Understandably.

"I can't believe she'd do this to Andrew," Riya says. "They're the perfect couple. And he's crazy in love with her!" She shakes her head. "Oh god, how is he taking this? He must be totally devastated."

I chew my lower lip. "Yeah, about that," I say. "He doesn't actually know that Laurel's left him yet. Shep and I have been trying to find her all morning so that I can fix this."

Riya holds up a finger. "Wait. You haven't told Andrew that she's called off the wedding?"

I shake my head.

She lets out a long breath. "Okay, okay. That's good," she says. "I think that was the right decision."

"You do?" My shoulders relax with relief. Riya's on our side. She's going to help us.

She nods. "You'll find Laurel and then he'll never have to

know that she almost left him at the altar," she says. "I'm sure that she just isn't thinking clearly and will hate herself for this when she comes to her senses."

Me too.

"Where have you checked so far?" she asks me.

"We've been to her apartment and my dad's hotel," I say. "We're going to the AGO next and then to High Park and maybe to Dufferin Grove. Can you think of anywhere else she might be hiding out?"

Riya drums her fingers on the counter. "The museum is a good idea," she says. "Laurel spends a lot of time there. Oh, and maybe check the Sharp Centre — it's right behind the museum. She works in the lobby sometimes, she says it inspires her." She thinks. "There's a bookstore not too far from High Park that she likes. She likes to browse there when she's stressed. I'll text you the address."

"That would be great. Thanks."

"Laurel really could be anywhere, though," Riya says, sighing. But then her face brightens. "Wait, did you try Friend Finder?"

I nod. "She's turned her phone off."

She frowns. "So that means she really doesn't want to be found."

Maybe. But I can't let that stop me from looking for her.

"She told my dad she just needed time to think," I say. I fill her in on their conversation at his hotel this morning as well as my theory about why Laurel left the note in her hotel room instead of in her apartment.

"You're right, it sounds like she's not sure that she's making the right decision," Riya says. "I feel terrible that she didn't think she could talk to any of us about this. Running away never solves anything, it just makes everything worse."

The bathroom door suddenly opens and Nathalie pokes her head in.

"What on earth is taking you guys so long?" she asks, irritably. "We've all been waiting for you for ages."

"Whoops, sorry," Riya says. "We just need one more minute and then we'll be right out."

Nathalie rolls her eyes and the door swings closed.

"I was supposed to meet Shep fifteen minutes ago, but I still have to figure out how to get away from my mom," I say.

"Don't worry about that, you leave her to me," Riya replies, with a small smile. "Now go and find our girl."

nine

RIYA CAME through and suggested to my mom and the other women that they all come shopping with her, leaving me an opening to volunteer to take lunch back to the Hazleton for my sister. My mom leapt at the chance — shopping is her favorite pastime — so odds are she won't be back to the hotel for hours, which means that I don't have to stress about her checking up on Laurel.

At least one thing went right today, I think as I hurry down the street on my way to meet Shep.

I catch sight of him through the crowd, waiting for me at our designated spot at the corner of Bay and Bloor, in front of The Gap. He looks like he just stepped out of one of their ads in his khaki shorts and white t-shirt, a light breeze ruffling his dirty blonde hair. I slow down, giving myself the freedom to check him out before he notices me. He is so hot that it makes it really difficult to see him as just a friend. If he were any other guy, I might throw away any hesitations and happily give in to this magnetic pull that he seems to have over me, but he's not just any other guy — he's

Laurel's almost brother-in-law, which could make things super messy. I'm fairly certain that my sister would not be thrilled if she knew that I like him and since I've already made her feel terrible enough this weekend Shep is definitely going to have to remain off-limits.

It doesn't matter, I tell myself. *All that matters is that I find Laurel.*

Shep glances up as I approach. He tucks his phone away, but not before I see the beautifully vibrant pink and blue colors of Lore Olympus on his screen. The fact that he looked up the comic based on my recommendation at dinner last night makes my heart swell.

"Hey," I say, suddenly nervous. "Sorry I'm so late. Lunch went on a lot longer than I expected and then it took me forever to get away."

"Don't worry about it," he replies and the smile he gives me makes me warm all over. It would sure be a lot easier to keep things strictly platonic if he didn't look at me like that.

I hand him the white bakery box of tea sandwiches and treats from the restaurant.

"What's this?" he asks.

I shrug. "I figured that you probably hadn't had a chance to eat yet."

"You figured right," he says, his smile widening as he opens the box and peeks inside. "Thanks Arden. That was so nice of you."

I smile back at him. I feel a little guilty for taking credit for bringing him lunch, considering that this food was really meant for my sister — and since my mom is the one who actually paid for it — but it's not like Laurel is going to eat it. I like that I've made him happy, so I decide there's no harm in keeping that bit of information to myself.

Shep lifts a bite-sized brownie cut into the shape of a star out of the box. "I thought we could take the subway to the AGO," he says. "Should only take us about fifteen minutes or so to get there."

I nod. "Okay."

As it turns out, the nearest subway station is a few blocks away. The street is lined with a ton of high-end stores that I know my mom loves and since Riya didn't tell me exactly where she was taking everyone, Shep and I detour down alleys and side streets to avoid an accidental run-in with them.

"So tell me what happened with the doctor," I say just as Shep pops the brownie into his mouth.

He finishes chewing and says, "Fortunately, the hotel didn't provide any information about who she was supposed to be treating, so I told her that my insanely over-protective mom had called because I had a headache but that I felt okay now and I was very sorry that we wasted her time." He looks over at me and I notice that he has a brownie crumb on his bottom lip. Looking at his lips makes me think of kissing. I wonder what he would he do if I just leaned over and planted one on him?

I shake my head. *Oh my god, what is wrong with me?*

"She was very nice about it," Shep adds. He digs in the pocket of his shorts and hands me a few crumpled bills — what remains of my spending money after he paid the doctor. "I told her that I'm Canadian, hoping that she wouldn't charge me — we have universal health care here so we don't pay to see the doctor — but I guess that doesn't include hotel visits. She made me sign a form, so you probably can't even get reimbursed on your medical insurance because my name is on the paperwork."

I shrug. My mom handles our insurance and there's zero chance I'd ever ask her to try to claim this visit. If I did, I'd have to explain what Shep was doing in Laurel's room and why I lied about her having a migraine.

"Canadian money is so pretty," I say, tucking the bills into my wallet. Each bill is a different color — blue, purple, red, brown — which makes it easy to tell the denominations apart. "They kind of remind me of euros."

"You've been to Europe?" he asks me.

I nod and drop my wallet back into my bag. "Greece. We went when I was twelve," I say, fiddling with Laurel's evil eye bracelet on my wrist. Life went downhill pretty quickly after we got home from that vacation, even though my parents didn't actually separate for another few torturous years.

Shep nudges me. "Is that why you're so into mythology?"

I nod. "It's the place where it all began." In the weeks leading up to that trip, I read everything I could get my hands on about Greece — travel guides, history books, even a biography on Nana Mouskouri, an old-timey famous Greek singer — but it was the myths that really stuck with me.

"So, just out of curiosity, what is it about Greek mythology that you find so interesting?" Shep says.

I blink at him. I mean, where do I even start? What *isn't* interesting about Greek mythology?

"Well, I mostly like the stories themselves — they're,

like, ancient soap operas, full of romance and drama. They've been passed around for *thousands* of years and people are still interested in hearing them today. That's pretty incredible," I say. I can hear myself talking faster, my words tripping over each other in my excitement.

I glance over at Shep to see if he's still interested — I've been known to get carried away talking about this subject, long after the person I'm talking to has grown bored — but he nods encouragingly, so I decide to keep going.

"And it's pretty cool that you can see the influence of Greek mythology pretty much everywhere in the world if you know where to look," I say, pointing at the Starbucks across the street. "The mermaid in their logo is based on a siren, which are these sexy mermaids who lure sailors by singing to them."

"And now they lure us to drink coffee," he says with a laugh.

I smile. "I guess they do."

I continue as Shep devours an egg salad sandwich. "Nike is another example," I say. "One of the world's biggest athletic companies and it was named after the Greek goddess of victory. That swoosh in their logo represents her wing."

"Now that you mention it, that swoosh does kind of look like a wing," Shep says, reaching for the last treat in the box, a tiny lemon tart. "And I think there's quite a lot of Greek mythology in superhero movies."

I grab his arm. "Yes! Superman is like Zeus. Wonder Woman is based on Artemis, a Greek goddess. And all the Justice League characters are based off the Olympians, too."

"Wow, you really know your stuff," Shep says. "We went

to Crete when I was four or five but I don't remember much about it, other than the water was so clear and so incredibly blue. I've never seen anything like it."

"The Aegean Sea," I reply, dodging a guy on a skateboard. "Named after Aegeus, who, according to Greek legend, threw himself off a cliff and drowned in the ocean when he thought his son was dead."

"Let me guess, plot twist, his son was still alive."

I nod. "Yep. It was a total misunderstanding," I say. "Long story, but basically, Theseus — that's Aegeus's son — sailed off to Crete to end this totally psycho practice of sacrificing people to a minotaur—"

"That's the monster with the head of a bull, body of a man?" he asks.

"Yes," I say. "Anyway, Theseus does the job and kills the Minotaur with his bare hands, then sets sail back to Athens a hero. Unfortunately, in all of the celebrating, Theseus forgot that before he left on his big, Minotaur-slaying adventure, his father had asked him to swap out the black sail on his ship for a white one. That way, when Theseus sailed into the habor, his dad would immediately know that he was alive and well. But when the ship showed up with that black flag instead—"

"Aegeus thought his son was dead," Shep says. He smiles at me. "Who needs college? You already sound like a professor."

I blush. "Hopefully one day I will be," I say. "Although professors have to do a lot of public speaking and, as you may have noticed last night, I'm not exactly awesome at it." It probably goes without saying that I would rather do almost anything else than get up in front of an audience, which is definitely going to present a problem for me in the future if I want to teach.

"I used to have terrible stage fright, before I started busking," he says. "The only way really get over it is to just do it over and over and over again, until it doesn't bother you anymore. I don't even really think about it now."

I can't imagine a day when standing in front of an audience won't bother me. Just the thought of being the centre of attention and having everyone staring at me makes my palms start to sweat.

"Oh, I forgot to tell you, Riya thinks we should check the Sharp Centre, too, since it's right behind the museum," I tell Shep as we reach the subway station, watching as he walks over and tosses the take-out box in a garbage can. "And also Dufferin Grove, the neighborhood where she and Laurel used to live."

Shep stops dead and turns to stare at me, his eyebrows drawing together. "You told Riya about Laurel?"

I blink, taken aback by his tight expression. "I had to," I say. "I needed her help to get away from my mom. And she's my sister's best friend...I thought she might be able to give us some insight about where Laurel might have gone."

Shep scrubs his hand through his hair. "This is getting out of hand. All these people know that Laurel's taken off, but my brother still has no idea."

My stomach drops. "I guess I didn't think of it that way."

I probably should have, but I didn't.

Shep sighs. "Arden, what are we doing? If we don't find Laurel — and let's be realistic, there's a very strong possibility that we won't find her — Andrew will kill me for not telling him about all of this sooner. And I wouldn't blame him. This is his life, his *future* that we're talking about — he should know what's going on. If I was him, I'd want to know."

"We're going to find her, don't worry," I reassure him. I can't let him give up hope. If he decides that he's out and that we really do have to tell his brother, then there's zero chance that I'll find Laurel. And I can't do this without his help.

"We're doing this for Andrew. We have his best interests at heart," I say. "We're trying to prevent a disaster."

"This is already a disaster," he replies, crossing his arms. "What's going to change if we find her? We can't talk her into something that she doesn't want to do."

"We're not going to," I say. "We're going to tell her that she needs to talk to him, face to face. Andrew deserves that." It's the very least he deserves.

And if we don't find my sister, then I can only hope that he'll understand that we were just trying to help. My stomach tightens. Hopefully he'll somehow be able to find it in his heart to forgive me for ruining his wedding — even if I'll never be able to forgive myself.

Shep still doesn't look convinced.

"Riya promised me that she wouldn't tell anyone what's going on," I add, my heart racing. "And besides, the more people we have out looking for Laurel, the better chance that we'll find her. My dad and Rachel are searching for her now, too." As I was walking over to meet Shep, I started a text thread with Riya and my dad to keep them up to date. Riya's already sent a list of Laurel's favorite places near the waterfront, and my dad volunteered to go down there to see if he could spot her.

Shep's eyes narrow. "Wait. Rachel knows that Laurel's missing, too?"

"I mean...yeah," I say, feeling my cheeks flush. "She was there when Laurel showed up at their hotel this morning." I guess I forgot to mention that. "But that's it. Just Riya, my dad and Rachel. And the two of us."

He sighs again. "I really hope that I don't regret this," he says, but his face relaxes a tiny bit. Relief flows through me as he steps forward and holds open the glass door for the subway station.

ten

MY HEART STARTS to slow to its normal rhythm as we head to the turnstile at Museum station. We hold our PRESTO passes against the card readers. The light changes to green, the silver gates slide open and we walk through to the other side.

We take the escalator down. At the bottom, Shep turns right for the southbound platform, which is swarmed with people waiting for the next train.

"Wow, those sculptures are really cool," I say, studying the carvings on the columns — an ivory-colored Egyptian sarcophagus, a totem of a bear and a few that even look like ancient Greek columns, like something you'd see on the Acropolis.

"Yeah, they are," Shep replies as we nudge our way through the crowd to a spot near the end of the platform. "This is the stop for the Royal Ontario Museum. They added the sculptures a bunch of years ago when they renovated the station to reference the exhibits. The Toltec Warrior is my favorite."

I nod and fan my face with my hand. As beautiful as this station is, it's stifling hot down here — much hotter than it is outside, and that's saying something — and the combination of the terrible, suffocating humidity and the stench of a million sweating bodies packed together like sardines is truly its own special hell.

Shep and I haven't spoken in a few minutes and the longer the silence between us stretches, the more my nerves start to amp up again. I don't know him well enough yet to read his moods. I keep sneaking glances at him, trying to determine whether he's still upset with me for telling Riya about Laurel, but he doesn't seem mad, just lost in thought.

Thankfully, the train soon rumbles into the station, slowing to a stop alongside the platform. The doors hiss open and a bunch of people spill out. Shep and I squeeze on with the rest of the crowd and I'm relieved to feel the blast of air-conditioning. There aren't any available seats, so we end up standing very close together — which I have to admit I don't hate — our arms extended into the air so we can clutch the metal bar to keep from falling over when the train starts to move.

"So tell me another story, Professor," Shep says as we pull out of the station. I'm thrown by the non-sequitur at first, but then I realize that he's just picking up our earlier conversation.

"Okay, let's see." I think for a minute, trying to decide which of my favorite myths to share with him. "Have you heard of Persephone and Hades?"

"King and Queen of the Underworld," he says and I remember that he was reading Lore Olympus when we met up earlier.

"That's them," I say, nodding. "So their story starts when Hades developed this huge crush on Persephone, even though she was his niece—"

"Ew, what?" Shep's face screws up in disgust. "Hades had a thing for his niece?"

"I know. It's twisted." But that's the Greek gods for you. They were a messy bunch. "Anyway, he kidnapped her and took her to the Underworld and forced her to marry him. Persephone wasn't thrilled about this, naturally, but Hades figured he would win her over and make her love him by giving her a bunch of gifts. Not surprisingly, that didn't work. She hated his guts for taking her away from her mother, Demeter."

The train stops at the next station and Shep shuffles a little closer to me as more people get on.

'Now, what Persephone didn't realize was that her dad, Zeus, was in on everything. Hades was his brother and he'd allowed him to take her—"

"Wait. Her dad *let* him kidnap her?"

I nod. "Eventually, Zeus stepped in to try and handle the situation, but only because his wife wasn't pulling out of her depression. Demeter was the goddess of agriculture and when Persephone disappeared she stopped caring for the earth and people started to die of starvation, which was obviously a big problem."

"Obviously," he says.

I notice an older woman sitting across the aisle listening to me tell the story. Feeling awkward, I lower my voice to an almost whisper. "Zeus wanted to keep his brother and his wife happy, so he decided that he'd let each of them spend six months a year with Persephone."

"So Persephone was stuck with Hades for half a year, every year, even though she hated him?"

"Well, she eventually grew to love him, so I guess maybe it wasn't too bad."

Shep raises an eyebrow. "She grew to love the guy who kidnapped her? Like she had Stockholm Syndrome?"

"Probably," I say. "Anyway, they stayed together, even if they both ended up cheating on each other. The Greek gods weren't super into monogamy."

I tell him about Nyx, goddess of the night, and Dionysius, god of wine and parties, who was taken from his mother's womb by his father — also Zeus — and carried around in his thigh until he was ready to be born.

Shep shakes his head. "That's weird."

"That's nothing. One time, Zeus had a terrible headache and so his friend Hephaestus pried open his skull with a sword and out popped Athena, Zeus's daughter, fully grown and wearing armor. Turned out that he'd eaten his pregnant wife Metis years before and the baby had grown in his forehead."

"Of course it did," Shep says. "Wait. I thought Zeus was married to Demeter?"

"He was," I say. "He had seven wives. Demeter, Metis, Eurynome. One of them — Hera — was his sister."

Shep stares at me. "He married his sister?"

I nod. "I told you it's twisted."

The train suddenly lurches. I sway on my feet and when Shep grabs my arm to steady me, a little zip runs up my spine. I know he feels it, too, because a blush travels all the way up his neck and spreads across his cheeks. A thousand butterflies start to flap their wings in my stomach.

Our eyes meet. Shep swallows and drop my arm. "This is our stop," he says, as the train rolls into St. Patrick's station.

It seems impossible that Shep and I have only known each other such a short amount of time — less than a day! — and even more impossible that I have such a strong connection to someone I barely know. But the feelings are there and as much as I'm trying to put them aside for my sister's sake and focus on the task at hand, that's proving to be a lot easier said than done.

I try and shake off the feelings as we get off the train and head up the escalator and out onto Dundas street. As we start to walk towards the art gallery I spot the CN Tower in the distance, peeking out from between the buildings.

"Tallest structure in Canada," Shep says, following my gaze. "Used to be the tallest in the world, before the Canton Tower in China was built. And then came the Tokyo Skytree, so now we're in third place." We stop at the crosswalk to wait for the light to change. "I like to think of the CN Tower as a compass," he adds. "It's at the south end of the city and since you can see it from almost anywhere in the downtown core it makes it easy to tell which direction you're going."

"So that means we're heading west," I say.

Shep glances at me and smiles. "Exactly right."

The light changes and we cross the street. I study the AGO as we approach — the building is beige and rather plain, aside from the long, impressively huge sail-like glass panel jutting out of the top.

"This is my favorite building," he says. "Frank Gehry, the famous architect, worked on the museum's redesign several years ago. I'm a huge fan of his. He's a true artist — he designed the Dancing House in Prague and the Guggenheim in Spain. Someday I'm going to visit every one of his buildings."

We walk through a set of glass doors and into the gallery, passing by the gift shop. The line for tickets is depressingly long, but it snakes through a gorgeous spiral wooden structure, which is like an art piece in itself.

I look around the welcome area. It's a beautiful, calming space, filled with light and warm wood, from the floors to the ticket counter. "I've seen his binocular building in Venice Beach. It's pretty cool."

Shep nods. "Yeah, it is. Did you know that Gehry is Canadian?" he asks me as the line inches forward. "He was born right here in Toronto." His Canadian accent makes Toronto sound like "Tronno".

"I didn't know that, actually," I reply. "I know that Elliott Page is from here though. And Justin Bieber."

"Elliott Page is actually from Halifax. Justin Bieber grew up in Stratford, which is a small town a few hours from here," he says. "Wayne Gretzky and Seth Rogan and Celine Dion and that girl from The Vampire Diaries are all Canadian, too."

"Really? Which girl?"

"The one with the long dark hair," he says. "The main vampire, the one that the two brothers were always fighting over."

"Nina Dobrev," I say. Laurel and I watched every episode of The Vampire Diaries together when I was way too young to be watching it. "She was also on Degrassi."

His eyebrows rise. "You know about Degrassi?" he asks, clearly impressed.

"Of course." I binge-watched a bunch of seasons earlier

this summer in preparation for my trip. I came for the rare shots of the city and stayed for the high school melodrama and hard-won life lessons. "Zoe and Rasha forever," I add.

"I'm more of an OG fan myself," he says. "All the way with Stephanie Kaye."

I give him a blank look.

"Stephanie Kaye? Joey Jeremiah?" he asks, his brow furrowing. "Wheels?"

I shake my head.

"Trust me, go back and watch the original series from the '80s. I promise it won't disappoint."

I smile at him, realizing that I'm having fun, and then I quickly feel guilty again. I'm supposed to be focused on searching for my sister so that I can beg her forgiveness and try and repair the damage I've done, but if I'm honest with myself, as awful as I feel about Laurel and this whole situation, I'm also really enjoying spending time with Shep and seeing the city.

It's official: I'm the worst sister in the world.

We're almost at the front of the line. Shep pulls out his phone and opens Instagram, scrolling through Laurel's photos until he finds a picture of my sister — a closeup of her laughing into the camera, her strawberry blonde hair caught up in a messy bun, a constellation of freckles across her nose. She looks so happy, like she doesn't have a care in the world.

I wonder when that changed.

I take my wallet out of my bag, hoping that I have enough to cover our entry fee. I can't let Shep to pay for himself — he's already done so much and besides, it's my fault that we're in this situation.

"There's no charge for us to enter the gallery," he says to me. "Admission is free if you're under twenty-five. You'll just need to show your ID."

Perfect! After paying for the doctor visit, I'm running seriously low on funds. I intentionally left my debit card back in San Diego so that I wouldn't spend too much on this vacation.

A woman behind the glass partition beckons us forward.

"Hi," Shep says as we slide our student cards towards her.

"Good afternoon," she says, glancing at our IDs. As she taps something into the computer, I study the tattoos covering her arms — starfish and dolphins and a busty, blue-haired mermaid. Poseidon, God of the sea, rises angrily out of a wave, bare-chested and brandishing a spiky gold trident. I wonder if she knows that Poseidon was a crappy husband who cheated on his wife, Amphitrite, or if she just thought he would make a cool-looking tattoo (which he totally does). It's probably too personal to ask her, though.

"Here you go," the woman says, sliding a pair of tickets towards us through a hole in the partition.

"Actually, I was wondering if you could help us with something." Shep turns his phone around and holds the photo of Laurel up to the glass. "I was wondering if you've seen this girl."

"She's my sister," I add, so that she doesn't think we're total creeps. "We thought that she might be here."

The woman squints as she studies the photo. "Yeah, she comes in here a lot," she says and my heart leaps. "But I haven't seen her today. Then again, I just started my shift twenty minutes ago, so who knows."

Shep and I exchange a glance. It's still worth checking.

"One last question," he says to her. "Where can we find the painting of the red-haired woman in the nightgown? She has this really magnetic stare that kind of follows you around the room?" He turns to look at me. "Do you remember what the painting was called?"

I shake my head. I didn't think to write down the name of it. I'm about to pull out my phone to check my search history, when the woman says, "*The Marchesa Casati.*"

I smile. "Yes, that's it."

"She's on the first floor, gallery 137." The woman takes out a laminated map of the AGO and points to a room off a long hallway. "Go through these doors, hang a right and then take the second door on the left," she says, dragging her finger across the map to mark the route. "You have to walk through gallery 134 to get into 137 — you'll find the Marchesa on the wall on the right-hand side."

"Thank you," I say as Shep grabs our tickets.

We head into the main area, the hub of the gallery. We bypass the wide wooden staircases on either side that lead to the other floors and turn right. We speed-walk down a plum-colored hall lined with black-framed photos until we reach the second door on the left.

Several groups of people are in the first gallery, staring at gorgeous portraits of European royalty painted lifetimes ago, like the sullen King Henry VIII, a white fur and red velvet cloak thrown over his broad shoulders. I quickly scan the crowd for Laurel, but she's not here.

"No running," the security guard warns us as we enter the second gallery.

This room is almost empty and it's as quiet as a library.

My heart stops when I spot a girl with strawberry blonde hair and Laurel's same lithe frame standing at the other end of the room, but then she turns around and I realize that it's not my sister.

"Arden? The painting's over here," Shep says.

The Marchesa Casati is hanging on the wall in an ornate gold frame. She's bigger than I expected – at least twice the size of the print hanging in Laurel's apartment. I immediately get why Laurel is so drawn to this portrait — there's something so intriguing about the way the woman with the tousled red hair and dark eyes stares back at me, like she's studying me instead of the other way around. I take in her hands, folded neatly together and balanced on her hip, her creamy skin and swan-like neck, the way the collar of her nightgown dips daring low into her cleavage. She really is a masterpiece.

Shep leans forward to read the sign mounted next to her portrait. "Luisa Casati," he says. "Painted by Welsh artist Augustus John in 1919. Orphaned at the age of 15, the Marchesa was an Italian heiress, muse and performance artist, known for her eccentricities. She aimed to be a living work of art. Known as the 1920's answer to Lady Gaga, Casati wore lives snakes as jewellery, kept peacocks as pets and threw world-famous masquerade balls."

"I love that she didn't live a conventional life," I say, and it occurs to me that maybe that's why Laurel admires her, too — Luisa Casati was brave enough to do things her own way and on her own terms, during a time where women were only expected to be wives and mothers. And I recognize a little of the Marchesa in my sister — Laurel has always forged her own path, too. It's how she ended up in Toronto. It's also why she's run out on her own wedding.

I'd like to spend more time looking at the painting and learning more about the Marchesa's life but we still have four more levels to search, so, with a last look at her over my shoulder — those deep brown eyes watching me go — I follow Shep out of the gallery.

We manage to cover the rest of the AGO in fifteen minutes because we don't stop to look at any other art. We check every corner of the building for Laurel — the café on the bottom level, the walls of which are papered in a trippy black and white spiral pattern; Galleria Italia, a glass and wood tunnel that runs along the length of the second floor; the members lounge, a warm, cream-colored space with dark leather couches and a beautiful wood fireplace. We even check the gift shop.

But Laurel is nowhere to be found.

"Well, we knew that finding her here was a longshot," Shep says as I pay for a postcard of The Marchesa Casati. "Finding her at all is a longshot, actually. She could be anywhere in the city."

I don't want Shep to know that I'm losing faith too or he might try and convince me to give up again, so I smile at him and say, "Still a few more places on our list."

I know the odds of us stumbling across my sister at this point are not good, but that doesn't mean that I'm ready to stop looking for her. I still think that there's a chance, however small, that we'll find her. I have to believe that.

eleven

"WHAT TIME ARE we supposed to be at the rehearsal dinner?" Shep asks me as we leave the art gallery.

"Six thirty," I say.

He rubs his forehead, apprehension and stress written all over his face. "So that gives us just over three hours to try and find Laurel and convince her not to call off the wedding."

I nod, but my chest suddenly feels tight. Three hours isn't much time.

"You know, if by some miracle we actually do manage to find her, this still might all be for nothing," Shep continues. "We might not be able to convince her to talk to Andrew. And like I said before, I don't think that we should try and talk her into marrying him."

I shake my head. "I don't either."

"You really think that finding her is going to make a difference?" he asks.

I don't know. What I do know is that what I said in my speech last night pushed my sister over the edge and scared her off getting married. And I won't know whether that's a good thing or a bad thing until I talk to her.

"I know how much she loves your brother," I say, hoping that he doesn't pick up on the fact that I'm not really answering his question.

Shep lets out a weary sigh. "I just don't want him being blindsided at his rehearsal dinner. That's almost as bad as being left at the altar."

"We're not going to let that happen," I say. "If we don't find Laurel in the next hour and a half, then we'll tell him everything. Okay?" That will hopefully give us enough time to check the last few places on our list. If Laurel's not at any of them, then I'll give up. I'll have to.

He nods. "Okay."

Next stop is The Sharp Centre, which is part of the main campus of Ontario College of Design, Laurel's alma mater. Fortunately, it's located right behind the AGO so it takes us less than two minutes to walk there.

"Wow, okay," I say, as we turn the corner and I see a towering table-like structure — a massive black and white pixelated slab held aloft by half a dozen different colored legs. The structure partially covers a cement courtyard and hovers over a plain brown brick building.

"Yeah, you either love The Sharp Centre or you hate it," Shep replies. "I happen to love it."

"It's certainly different."

He smiles. "That's a polite way of saying you hate it."

I laugh. "I don't hate it." I don't understand it, but I don't hate it.

We walk into the lobby. A quick sweep proves that Laurel isn't here, either. There are many other places in this building where my sister could be hiding out, but Riya specifically mentioned that Laurel likes to work in the lobby and since we don't have time to check every room, I'm going to just cross The Sharp Centre off our list.

My feet are starting to hurt as Shep and I walk back towards Dundas to catch the bus to Dufferin Grove, the neighborhood where Laurel lived before she moved in with Andrew last year. I'm tired and sweaty and losing a bit more hope that we'll ever find my sister with every step.

"I need a drink," Shep says, stopping in front of a convenience store. "I can literally feel the sun sucking every last bit of moisture out of me. Do you want anything?"

I nod. "I could use some water." And I should probably reapply some sunscreen or pretty soon I'm going to be as red as a lobster — and that's not how I want to look in Laurel's wedding pictures. Assuming that we'll even get to take wedding pictures that is.

We pop into the store and Shep grabs two bottles of water from the cooler and a bag of chips while I pick up a bottle of SPF 30. At the counter, I open my bag to get my wallet, but he shakes his head.

"I've got this," he says.

"Thanks." I feel guilty about letting him pay — especially because the sunscreen is twelve dollars — but I give in because I only have forty dollars left and that has to last me the rest of the weekend.

The bus stop is right outside the store. As we wait in the glassed-in shelter, I rub some sunscreen on my arms while Shep opens the chips. He shoves a few into his mouth, crunching loudly, then shakes the bag in my direction. I close the cap on the sunscreen, drop it into my purse and reach for a chip.

I assume from the dark red color that they're BBQ flavor, but when I take a bite I discover that whatever this is, it isn't BBQ — it has a similar sweet and salty taste, but also a note of something weird that I can't quite put my finger on.

"What did I just put in my mouth?" I ask Shep, swallowing.

He flips his wrist, turning the bag so that I can see the blocky yellow print on the front.

"*Ketchup* chips?" I reply, wrinkling my nose. "Why? Why would someone do this?"

He raises his eyebrows. "You've never had ketchup chips before?"

"I've never even *heard* of ketchup chips before."

"Huh. Must be a Canadian thing," he says, shoving another handful into his mouth.

"They don't really taste anything like ketchup," I say, sticking my hand in the bag to grab another one. Actually, they're not that bad. Maybe they're an acquired taste. "I wonder what other food you have up here that we don't."

"Have you had poutine?" he asks. "That's a Quebec thing, although you can get it pretty much anywhere."

"Fries with gravy and cheese, right?"

Shep nods.

"Yeah, I've tried it," I say. "It's good."

"How about a Nanaimo bar?"

When I shake my head, his face lights up. "We definitely need to rectify that," he says. "Nanaimo bars are probably the best baked good ever invented."

"Okay, but what are they exactly?" I ask. The name tells me nothing.

"They're this coconut custard bar thingy with a layer of chocolate on top," he says, balling up the empty chip bag and depositing it in a nearby trash can. "I'm not selling it too well, but trust me, you'll love it."

"I don't know. I'm not big on coconut," I say.

His eyes widen. "What? How can you not like coconut?"

"Um, because I don't like it. It tastes like sunscreen."

"You've tried sunscreen?" He smiles.

I roll my eyes but I smile back at him.

"There's just a hint of it in Nanaimo bars," he says. "It's only in the crust. You *have* to try it."

"Okay, okay, I'll try one. For you."

We're flirting again. I'm flirting with him and he's flirting back, like this is just a regular day and we're just two regular people. But it isn't and we aren't. I shouldn't be having fun, I should be focused on finding my sister — that's the whole reason we're here, after all. For Laurel.

And so I look away from Shep, a now-familiar wave of guilt washing over me.

A minute later the bus arrives. The middle door hisses open and a crowd gathers in front of it. I scramble to dig my Presto pass out of my wallet — *why* didn't I take it out while we were waiting? As we join the line to board, Shep tells me not to worry about it.

"They don't usually check when it's this busy anyway," he says.

"Don't usually?" I whisper. "But what if they *do* check?"

He shrugs. "Then you show them your ticket. They're only going to fine you if you don't have a ticket."

He walks down the aisle to two seats at the back, standing aside so I can slip past him into the window seat. "So. Got any other twisted stories for me, Professor?" he asks, settling in beside me.

I set my bag at my feet, mentally cycling through all my favorite myths, debating which one to share with him. "Have you heard of Ariadne?"

He shakes his head and twists the cap off his water bottle.

"Remember Theseus? The guy who killed the minotaur with his bare hands?"

Shep nods and takes a drink of water, downing almost half the bottle in one long gulp.

"Okay, so when Theseus first arrived in town to slay the Minotaur, Ariadne, the King's daughter, took one look at him and fell instantly in love."

"As one does," he says.

"Now, this was kind of a sticky situation for Ariadne because the Minotaur was her brother," I say.

"Wait. Ariadne was okay with Theseus killing her brother?"

"Well, her brother was a minotaur and he was eating people, so yeah, she didn't have a problem with it," I say. "Although to be fair, the minotaur was just doing what minotaur's do. It was actually their father, King Minos, who was behind the idea to sacrifice people."

"So King Minos was a bad dude," Shep says.

"The worst dude," I reply. "Anyway, the minotaur lived inside a labyrinth, which was set up with all sorts of traps that could get you killed, and since Ariadne didn't want something bad to happen to her new boyfriend she gave him a spool of thread to help him find his way back out." I shift a little in my seat. "She also gave him a sword to kill the minotaur, but only after Theseus agreed to marry her and take her back to Athens with him."

"She bribed him into marrying her?"

"Basically," I say. "So fast forward a few hours — Theseus gets through the maze and kills the minotaur, then he and Ariadne set sail on his ship, bound for Athens. They're happy, they're in love, they have their entire future ahead of them, everything's great. Or it should be, right?"

I look at Shep and he nods.

"Unfortunately, Theseus soon realized that he wasn't super into Ariadne after all," I say. "And he certainly didn't want to marry her."

My heart drops as soon as the words leave my mouth. Maybe this isn't the best myth to share with Shep, considering that my sister has basically pulled a Theseus, but I'm too far into the story to quit without it being super obvious.

I clear my throat. "So when the ship stopped on an island one night, Theseus decided that it was time to ditch her."

"Stand-up guy," Shep says.

"Total creep," I agree. "The next morning, when Ariadne woke up, she discovered that the ship had left without her. She was so angry and upset that she placed a curse on Theseus that made him forget to change the sails — remember I told you that his father asked him to replace the black sail with a white one so that he'd know that Theseus was alive?"

"Right. His father saw the black sail instead and threw himself into the ocean."

I nod.

"Okay, but why not curse Theseus directly?" Shep asks me. "Why bring his father into it?"

"Good question," I say. "I'm not sure. Maybe she knew that it would be worse for him, knowing that he'd have to live with the guilt of being indirectly involved in his father's death." I feel a sudden stab of sympathy for Theseus — if things don't work out the way I hope they will, then I'm going to have to learn to live with what I've done, too. And that's not going to be easy.

Shep's quiet for a moment. "What happened to Ariadne in the end? Did she ever get off the island?"

"In some versions of the myth she did," I say. "One story has her rescued by Dionysus, the god of wine, a few days later. They got married and live happily ever after."

"And the other stories?"

"Didn't end so well," I reply. "She always marries Dionysus, but her fate seems to change with each version — in one, she was turned to stone, in another she died during childbirth."

"Why are there so many different versions of the same myth?" he asks.

I shrug. "A lot of the myths have different versions. I guess because, over the years, there were so many different people telling them."

"Like an ancient game of telephone."

I smile at him. "Yes, kind of like that. Or they were adapted to fit a different culture or belief."

The bus ride takes longer than I expect it to, although Shep and I spend most of the time talking. With each mile, I find myself liking him more and more by the time we get off at Gladstone Avenue, I know that my heart's in trouble. I give up on telling myself that we aren't a good idea, that there's no sense in developing deep feelings for someone who lives thousands of miles away, because it's already too late for that. I am smitten.

I'm also not the only one. Unless I'm reading his signals totally wrong, I think Shep likes me, too. He's walking close enough to hold my hand — our fingers occasionally brush — and I have to really concentrate in order to keep my breath even. Neither of us is quite brave enough to make the first move.

We're both quiet as we pass through a leafy neighborhood lined with old houses in various stages of upkeep. Laurel's former residence is a crumbling red-brick Victorian with peeling white gingerbread trim located right across the street from a library. It isn't the worst house on the block but it's pretty darn close.

"This place is definitely haunted," I say.

Shep glances at me. "Do you believe in ghosts?"

"I don't not believe in them." I've never seen one personally, but that doesn't mean that they don't exist. And if they do, then I'm almost certain that they're hanging out in the basement of this house.

"It does have a sort of Amityville vibe to it," he says, turning back to stare at the house. "Maybe it's nicer on the inside."

It has to be. Not that we're going to ever see the inside of this place. My sister doesn't live here anymore, obviously — someone else rents it now and I'm not about to knock on the door. What would be the point? Now that I think about it, what is the point of even being here? Did I really expect that

I'd find Laurel lurking around outside a house she lived in more than a year ago? Then again, Riya did tell me that my sister loves this neighborhood and sometimes still visits, so I guess this is as good a place as any.

"Laurel wanted Andrew to move here," Shep says. "Not here to this house, but somewhere in this area, but he didn't want to break his lease. And their apartment is closer to his work."

"I didn't know that," I say. But that's not exactly surprising — there's so much that I don't know about my sister's life now, so much that she hasn't shared with me. I wonder how she felt, giving that up for Andrew. My sister has always been extremely independent, but things change when you're in a relationship. There's another person to consider. It can't always be about what you want.

"Riya told me there's a bookstore nearby that Laurel likes to go to," I say. "The Monkey's Paw." I take out my phone and map out the address Riya sent me.

"That's just a couple of blocks away from here," he says, looking at the map.

I take a last look at Laurel's old house and then we continue down the street.

"Have you ever read The Monkey's Paw?" Shep asks me.

I shake my head. "I don't think so."

"It's a really old story," he says, pushing a lock of dark blonde hair out of his eyes. "We had to read it in grade eight English class, but it's always stuck with me. Basically, this guy has this severed monkey's paw—"

I wrinkle my nose. "Gross."

"So gross. The thought of that severed paw always makes me wonder what happened to the rest of the monkey," he says. "Anyway, for some reason, I forget why, this thing grants its owner three wishes...but the trade-off is that while your wish will come true, it also comes with some really freaky consequences. Like the main character is this guy who wishes for two hundred bucks so that he can pay off his mortgage and he gets it, but only after his oldest son is killed in an accident at the factory where he works."

We turn left onto a busy street with lots of charming little stores, restaurants and bars. I peek into every shop that we pass, hopeful that I'll spot my sister, but of course, I don't see her. My anxiety starts to rise again. We are quickly running out of places to check.

"As you can imagine, when the guy's wife hears that their son is dead, she completely loses it," Shep continues. "But the man still has two more wishes left, so he thinks, no problem, I'll just use my second wish to bring my kid back to life. And he does and the son returns, but he's not really their son, he's still kind of dead, all mutilated and starting to decompose. So then the guy is forced to use his third and final wish to send him back to the grave."

"Be careful what you wish for," I murmur, my stomach tightening. It's a story that's currently playing out right before my own eyes: my sister wanted to get married, but when faced with the reality of walking down the aisle tomorrow she realized that it isn't what she wants after all. The name of the bookstore obviously triggered Shep's memory of reading this story, but I think he's also drawn the same conclusion about my sister because the air around suddenly feels charged with tension.

"That sounds very similar to the myth of King Midas," I add hastily, hoping to steer us away from a conversation about Laurel in case he changes his mind again about helping me find her. "Midas had a pretty baller lifestyle but he was super greedy and he wanted more, so he asked his friend Dionysus to give him the ability to turn anything he touched into gold."

"Dionysus? Isn't he the guy who married Ariadne?" Shep asks.

I nod. "A lot of the gods and goddesses show up in each other's stories."

"Sort of like the Marvel universe."

"Yeah. Sort of like that." I sneak a glance at him. His face is tight but he gives me a small smile. "Anyway, Midas thought that this was the greatest gift ever until he tried to eat and all his food turned to gold. He ended up nearly starving to death."

"I feel like that would be an easy enough fix," he says. "I mean, the guy was a king — he could have had someone feed him. Or he could have just worn gloves."

"Okay, you're right, he might have been able to work around that," I reply. "But then he hugged his daughter and turned her to gold."

"Yeah, I can see how that would be a problem."

"After that, he begged Dionysus to release him from the curse," I say. "Dionysus felt sorry for him so he agreed. Everything that King Midas had touched returned to normal, including his daughter."

"I hope Midas learned his lesson."

"He did. In fact, the whole experience made him a much better person. He was no longer such a greedy jerk and he shared his wealth with his kingdom."

Shep gently nudges me with his elbow. "You know,

you're a really good storyteller," he says. "And you're going to make a really great professor, Professor."

My cheeks flush. There's a lot more to working in academia than just telling stories, of course, but it feels so good to hear that he thinks I'm good at this part of it. I'm well versed in Greek mythology, I know all of the stories off-by-heart, but I've never actually shared them with anyone before. Not like I have with him. It just strengthens my resolve to stand up to my dad and tell him that I'm not going to be a lawyer.

Shep stops suddenly in the middle of the sidewalk and looks up at a sign above a small shop. "We're here," he says. "This is the place."

twelve

I STARE at the display of quirky sci-fi and classic horror books in the window of The Monkey's Paw, figuring that Riya must have been mistaken — this is a speciality bookstore, not the type of place that would interest Laurel at all. My sister is really more the mainstream fiction/celebrity memoir type.

Shep points at a creepy stuffed black raven perched on top of an old typewriter. "Do you think that's a reference to that Edgar Allen Poe poem?"

"The Raven?"

He nods.

"Yeah, I think it might be." My stomach flips. Ravens are an omen, a sign of bad luck. And we certainly don't need any more of that today.

The bell above the door rings as we step across the threshold. The bookstore isn't very big, it's just one long, open room lined with dark wood shelves that are crammed with books, a few well-worn oriental rugs thrown over highly polished wood floors. A handful of customers are browsing and a quick glance confirms that Laurel isn't among them. Because of course she isn't.

A very good-looking Japanese guy in thick tortoiseshell glasses gives us a welcoming smile from behind the counter. He's wearing suspenders over a white t-shirt that features a cartoon dinosaur in an old-fashioned bonnet.

"Brontësaurus," I say, pointing at his t-shirt.

His smile widens. "You got it."

"I wrote a paper on Jane Eyre last year," I say. "It's one of my favorite books."

"Oh yeah? Mine too," he says, bending forward and leaning his elbows on the counter. "I could talk about the Bronte sisters all day. Have you read The Tenant of Wildfell Hall? That book was fire! I really don't think that Anne gets the credit she deserves."

I'm about to agree with him when Shep clears his throat to remind me that I'm actually not here to talk books with a handsome stranger, I'm here to try and find my sister.

"Actually, we were wondering if you could help us," I say as Shep holds up his phone to show the guy the photo of Laurel. "We're looking for someone and we heard that she comes here sometimes. Have you seen her today?"

The guy's brow furrows. "You're looking for Laurel Stewart?"

"You know her?" I ask, my heart starting to beat a little faster.

He nods. "Yeah, she's a friend of mine. I haven't seen her in a few days, though." His face suddenly flushes a deep red and he starts to fiddle with his one of his suspenders. I'm wondering what to make of his reaction when he frowns and says, "Wait. Why are you looking for her?"

"Because she's missing," Shep says.

"Not like *missing* missing," I say quickly. I don't want to alarm him. "She's okay" — I think — "she's just kind of gone off the grid today and it's really important that we find her."

The guy takes a closer look at me. "Hey, are you Arden?"

I nod.

"I'm Kaito," he says, placing his hand on his chest, his grin widening.

It's pretty clear that he expects me to know who he is but as far as I can recall Laurel has never mentioned him. But I guess that's not too surprising — it's not like my sister and I have had any deep conversations in the past few years. I barely knew that Natalie, Riya and Charlotte existed before she got engaged, so it makes sense that Laurel has all sorts of friends she never told me about.

"Kaito, of course," I say, because I don't want to embarrass him by admitting that I don't know who he is. "It's so good to finally meet you."

"Laurel has told me so much about you," Kaito says warmly. "I feel like I know you already."

I blink at him, momentarily thrown off balance. I can't imagine what my sister would even tell him — our lack of communication goes both ways and I haven't told her much about my life, either. The idea that this guy that I've just met knows anything about me makes me super uncomfortable, especially when I know nothing about him.

An older woman brings a stack of books up to the

counter. Shep draws me away so Kaito can ring the purchase up for her but also so that he won't overhear us talking.

"Do you think that guy is the reason Laurel cancelled the wedding?" he whispers, his eyes full of worry.

"What?" I shake my head, but I sneak a glance at Kaito and my chest tightens. "No way."

It never even crossed my mind that this is all happening because Laurel might have feelings for someone else. But Kaito is unbelievably hot and he seems really nice and he did blush when he said they were friends and *oh god*, what if my sister doesn't want to marry Andrew because she's actually in love with this guy instead?

"She wouldn't do that to your brother," I add, wanting to believe that, but my voice wavers. Maybe Laurel would do that. What do I know? I mean, it would be pretty hypocritical if she left Andrew for someone else, considering how angry she's been about my dad's supposed affair with Rachel.

Shep doesn't look convinced. "It's pretty obvious that this Kaito guy has a thing for her," he says, crossing his arms.

"It's not obvious," I say. "And he said they're friends."

He rolls his eyes.

"But even if it is true and he does like her, that doesn't mean she feels the same way about him."

He shrugs. "Look at the facts. Laurel has already cancelled the wedding. She gave the ring back," he says. "We're just wasting our time on this wild goose chase, but even if we somehow find her it isn't going to make a difference. It won't change anything."

"We don't know that for sure," I insist. I still think that

she's just scared. "We can't quit now. We only have one more place on our list."

Shep shakes his head. "If it turns out that she's involved with this guy then I'm out, Arden. I mean it."

"Okay," I say. I can't fault him for that. And honestly if Laurel *is* cheating on Andrew then I'm out too. She'll be on her own.

Kaito finishes with the customer and gestures for us to come over to talk to him.

"So back to Laurel," he says. "What makes you think she's MIA?"

I don't want to tell him what's really going on — I don't know if he's friends with Charlotte or Nathalie or anyone else coming to the wedding and I don't want the news that my sister has run off to get back to them, obviously — so I just say that she isn't answering her phone and I'm worried about her.

Kaito gives me a strange look, like he doesn't quite buy it — and why would he? It sounds insane, searching for someone just because they've missed a few phone calls. I wish I was better at thinking on my feet.

"Do you know where she might be?" I ask him.

"No, but I'm probably the last person she'd tell," Kaito says with a frown.

What does that mean? "I thought you guys are friends."

"We are." He blushes again. "Or we were. She hasn't returned any of my texts in over a week," he says. "I, uh, did something kind of dumb."

I stare at him, my heart sinking. Beside me, Shep stiffens.

Kaito lets out a long breath and scrubs his hand through

his dark hair, a guilty expression crossing his (gorgeous) face. "I told her that I was in love with her," he says. "I know it's not cool to make a move on some other dude's fiancé, but I couldn't just let her get married without letting her how I feel about her."

"Yes, you could have," Shep growls at him and pounds his fist on the counter. "That other dude is my brother! Laurel dumped him and called off the wedding because of you!"

Kaito's eyebrows shoot up. "She did?"

"We don't know that she called it off because of him," I say to Shep, hoping to calm him down. "We won't know anything until we talk to her."

"You know what? I've heard enough," Shep says, fuming. He turns on his heel and stalks out of the shop, slamming the door behind him.

I watch him go, nervous that he's going to renege on our deal and call Andrew. I'm about to follow after him when Kaito says, "For what it's worth, Laurel doesn't feel the same way about me. She told me that she really loves her fiancé and that she only thinks of me as a friend."

My shoulders relax a little. I'm relieved to hear that my sister didn't cheat on Andrew. Not only that, but she's still in love with him.

Kaito gives me a small, sad smile. "Believe it or not, I just want Laurel to be happy," he says. "And she's made it very clear that's it won't be with me."

I know I shouldn't feel bad for him — what he did is kind of scummy — but it can't be easy knowing that the person you're in love with is going to marry someone else. I guess I can't blame him for not want to go through life wondering 'what if'.

"Please don't tell anyone that Laurel cancelled the wedding," I say to him. "Her fiancé doesn't know what's going on and I don't want him to find out."

"Isn't he going to notice when she doesn't show up at the church?"

"Not if I find her and talk to her first," I say.

Kaito nod. "Well, don't worry — there's no one for me to tell, we don't have any friends in common. And I think I've done enough damage anyway."

"Can you try sending her another message?" I know I'm grasping at straws but maybe she'll respond to him this time. Shep and I only have one more place to check before we call it quits.

"I'll try, but to be honest I think she's blocked me." He pulls out his phone and taps out a quick text. He's just pressed send when a man comes up and asks for a couple of tokens for the book vending machine. Kaito reaches into the till and exchanges the man's five-dollar bill for two silver coins. The man takes the coins and heads towards a retro looking turquoise and white machine wedged in the corner at the back of the store.

"You have a book vending machine?" I ask, my eyes widening.

Kaito nods. "Yup. It's pretty cool. Here, why don't you try it." He takes out another token and passes it to me. "On the house."

I thank him and give him my phone number on the off chance that Laurel does respond to him and then I walk over, open the door and stick my head outside. Shep's slumped against the building, his hands stuffed in the pockets of his shorts. I'm relieved to see that he's not on his phone.

"Come back inside," I say. "I want to show you something."

He scowls at me. "No way."

"Come on," I say. "Please? You have to see this."

"I'm not going back in there."

I sigh and walk over to him. "Look, Kaito told me that Laurel doesn't feel the same way about him," I say. "I really don't think that he's the reason she cancelled the wedding."

Shep looks at me, slightly mollified. "I still hate that guy."

"Fine, hate him, but we have, like, fifteen minutes to kill before the bus arrives and it's way too hot out here and I have a free token for the book vending machine," I say, smiling at him. "We can't leave here without trying it."

"A book vending machine?"

I nod.

"Okay, okay," he says.

He follows me back inside, shooting a nasty glance at Kaito as we pass by him. Excitement zips up my spine as we walk to the back of the store.

"Biblio-mat," Shep says, reading the big black letters written across the top of the machine.

"Every book a surprise," I read. "No two alike. Collect all 112 million titles."

"There's no way there's 112 million books inside this thing," he says.

I shrug. He's right, there's no way that's possible, but what does it matter? That doesn't make it any less amazing.

I insert the token into the slot, holding my breath as the machine rumbles and noisily spits a book into the compartment below. I lean down and pick it up. The cover is yellow with an orange and black butterfly, its wings spread wide.

"The Diving Bell and the Butterfly," I say.

"Never heard of it," Shep replies.

"That's what makes this vending machine so great," I say. "This probably isn't a book that either of us would have come across otherwise."

The author is someone named Jean-Dominique Bauby. I flip the book over and Shep huddles closer to me so that we can read the back cover copy together. It turns out that this is a memoir written back in the mid '90s by a French man who suffered a massive stroke and found himself imprisoned inside his own body.

"He dictated the entire book, letter by letter, by blinking his left eyelid?" Shep reads, shaking his head. "That's incredible."

It is incredible.

"You should take it," I say.

"Nah

"No, it's yours," he says. "On the condition that you read it and tell me exactly how the story turns out."

"Okay." I smile at him as I slip the book into my bag. Secretly, I'm thrilled — clearly this is a sign that Shep wants to stay in touch after I leave Toronto, even if Laurel doesn't go through with the wedding tomorrow. Of course, if she does marry Andrew, then it would make it even easier for us to stay connected.

Shep glances at his phone. "We'd better get going. If we miss the bus then we'll have to wait twenty minutes for the next one."

"Yeah, I guess we'd better." We can't lose any more time waiting — there's only a few hours left until the rehearsal dinner. My stomach clenches. I don't want to think about what we're going to have to do if Laurel isn't at High Park.

I say goodbye to Kaito on our way out of the bookstore but Shep completely ignores him. As we walk towards the bus stop, I rummage around in my bag for my wallet so I can have my Presto pass ready, but I can't find it. My heart starts to pound hard as I sift through all of the other items in my bag.

Oh no. *Oh no.*

I stop walking, trying to keep my breath even so I don't hyperventilate.

"Arden? What's wrong?" Shep asks.

"My wallet's missing," I say.

His eyebrows draw together. "What? Are you sure?"

I nod. Tears press against my eyes as Shep takes my arm and gently leads me over to a small patio attached to an Italian café. I sit down in one of the wrought iron chairs while he dumps everything in my bag onto the table — the new book, a bottle of water, the sunscreen, the postcard of The Marchesa Casati, my phone, the envelope containing Laurel's note to Andrew and her engagement ring, and the small, tiffany-blue wrapped present that Shep brought to her hotel room this morning.

But no wallet.

I groan and put my head in my hands. It really sucks to lose forty dollars but it sucks even more to lose all my ID.

My mom is going to kill me.

"Okay, let's think this through," Shep says. "Where did you use it last?"

I close my eyes and cast my mind back over the day. "The art gallery gift shop," I say. I see myself paying for the Marchesa Casati postcard. I open my eyes and look at Shep. "I think I might have left it sitting on the counter."

"Well that's easy enough to check," he says calmly. He takes out his phone, looks up the number for the AGO gift shop and calls them. "Hi, my friend was in your gift shop about forty-five minutes ago and she thinks she might have left her wallet behind." His eyes flick to me as he listens to the person on the other end speak.

"What does it look like?" he asks me.

"Dark blue with white stripes." Laurel gave me that wallet for Christmas last year, which makes me feel even worse about losing it.

Shep smiles at me. "It's there."

I let out a long, shaky breath. Disaster averted!

"That's great, thank you," he says into the phone. "We'll be by as soon as we can to pick it up." He hangs up and rests his hand on my shoulder. "They're going to keep your wallet behind the counter, but the museum closes in just over an hour. What do you want to do?"

I grimace. If we go all the way back to the AGO now then we'll have to give up searching for Laurel — there just isn't enough time to retrieve my wallet and then backtrack to High Park. And since it's the very last place on our list, I feel like we can't give up now.

"Let's just grab it on our way back to the hotel," I say. I start to shove my stuff back into my bag and my stomach drops as I suddenly remember why I was looking for my wallet in the first place.

"Shep. My Presto card is in my wallet," I tell him. I don't have any money on me either, so I can't even buy another transit pass.

He frowns. "Crap. I spent the last of my money on the chips and sunscreen," he says. "My wallet is so bulky, I hate carrying it around, so I just brought my Presto card and a twenty. I didn't think I'd need my bank card because I was just planning on delivering Laurel's present this morning and going back home."

I chew my thumbnail. "Should I just get on the bus and hope they don't check for my ticket?" It worked once, maybe it would work again. And it's not *really* stealing — I do have a valid pass. It's just not on me at the moment.

He shrugs. "We could probably risk it for the ride to High Park, but only if the bus is busy enough — if it's not, then the driver will definitely check," he says. "But even if we got away with it for the bus, we'll never pull it off on the subway. We need to take it back to the AGO and the stations are crawling with security guards."

My chest tightens. So we're stranded. Or I'm stranded, anyway — Shep still has his pass. Not that I think he'd just abandon me here.

"I guess I'd better call my dad," I say. "Maybe he can Venmo me."

I hate to do it, though. I don't like asking my father for anything because he doesn't believe in just handing me money — this is a big part of why I've been working since the minute I turned sixteen. This is a special circumstance, of course, but he'll want to know why I need it and when he finds out that it's because I've misplaced my wallet, well, I'll be listening to him lecture me about that for the rest of my life. But I don't see any way around it — I'm going to have to swallow my pride and ask him for help.

I guess Shep can tell that I'm less than thrilled about reaching out to my dad to save me because he smiles and says, "Don't call him just yet. I have an idea.

thirteen

"WHERE ARE WE GOING?" I ask Shep as he starts walking in the opposite direction of the bus stop.

"To get you another Presto pass," he answers. He's moving so fast that I have to double my steps to keep up with him.

"Oh yeah? And how are we going to do that?"

But he just gives me a mysterious smile and keeps walking.

We head down Bloor Street, past a Caribbean restaurant and a tattoo parlor. A few minutes later, Shep leads me through a set of wide glass doors and into the Dufferin subway station. We hurry across the cement floor, past a beautiful floor-to-ceiling mosaic of a faceless young woman in a red dress.

"I thought you said that we'd never get away with taking the train without a ticket?" I whisper, my blood pressure rising as I notice two transit security officers chatting near the stairs that I assume lead down to the subway platform. I automatically feel guilty and we're not even doing anything illegal yet.

"We're not taking the train," Shep replies.

"Then what are we doing here?"

"I told you, we're going to get you a pass." He walks by transit police and over to a girl about our age crouched over a guitar case covered in retro grunge band stickers.

"Camila," he says and the girl looks up. "I was hoping that I'd find you here."

She breaks into a wide smile and stands up. "Shephard Tremblay, where have you been hiding?" She throws her arms around him, squeezing him tight. My stomach drops as he laughs and hugs her back.

"Good thing you caught me, I was just about to leave," Camila says. She takes a step back to look him over. While she's busy doing that, I look her over: straight black hair falling in a shiny curtain to her waist, baggy beige cargo shorts, faded Pearl Jam t-shirt knotted just underneath her belly button. A gold guitar pick hangs from a leather cord around her neck. She's also wearing red high top converse sneakers, words written all over them in black Sharpie.

My chest tightens. Camila is pretty and cool and a fellow musician, exactly the type of girl I'd expect Shep to go for. I smooth a hand self-consciously over my hair, which is frizzing its way out of my ponytail, feeling as sweaty as if I'd just stepped out of a sauna.

"To be honest, I've been better," Shep tells her.

Camila shoots me a curious glance as he introduces me and explains my no money/misplaced wallet situation.

"I was hoping that you could do us a huge favor," he says.

I'm assuming that he's going to ask her if she'd be willing to lend him the money for my transit pass, which doesn't make me feel great — I know it's only a few dollars, but I wouldn't feel right taking money from a complete stranger, but instead Shep says, "Could I borrow your guitar for a few minutes?"

My breath catches. Wait. Is he planning to busk to raise money for my Presto pass?

I think he must be.

Camila nods. "Sure, of course," she says. "Anything to help."

She bends down again, flicks the latches open on her case, pulls out her guitar and hands it to him. "I should warn you, though, the crowd's pretty stingy today," she says. "I've been here for almost two hours and I've only got seventeen dollars to show for it."

"Fortunately, we don't need that much," Shep says, sliding the embroidered guitar strap around his neck. Camila positions the open case in front of his feet while he strums the strings a few times to warm up. He glances at me and the smile he gives me makes my heart start to race.

God, he is so hot. How is it possible to already have such strong feelings for someone I just met?

Camila and I move off to the side so we can watch him perform. I'm so focused on Shep's easy, relaxed stance and the expression of pure joy on his face as he plays that it takes me a minute to recognize the song, a slow, stripped-down version of Livin' on a Prayer.

I smile at the sound of his voice, deep and raspy, very old school rock and roll. He's good. Really good. Goosebumps all over my body good. I'm suddenly glad that I misplaced my wallet because if I hadn't then I might never have had the chance to hear him sing.

"Gives you the chills, right?" Camila whispers to me.

I nod, but I'm worried about the way that she's looking at him. Like she's super into him. Not that I blame her — why wouldn't she be interested? Not only is Shep good-looking, but he's also nice and funny and thoughtful, all of the qualities that make a great boyfriend.

I tense up. I hate the thought that he might be into her. The worst part is, I have no right to be jealous. I have no claim on Shep. Nothing has happened between us and there's a good chance that nothing ever will. *We're just friends*, I remind myself.

Still, I can't help hoping that he doesn't think of Camila that way. It's rotten of me, but that's how I feel.

As Shep continues to sing a wave of people walk past, hurrying to catch the next train or heading out onto the street, but a few of them look his way and a couple even throw change into Camila's guitar case.

A few minutes later, Shep brings the song to a close. He glances into the guitar case and frowns, then looks over at Camila.

"You're right, stingy crowd today," he says. "Bon Jovi usually brings me good luck, but I've only collected four dollars so far." He shrugs and his fingers start to strum the strings again. This time, I recognize what he's playing right away — Perfect by Ed Sheeran. Laurel and Andrew's wedding song.

Shep starts to sing again and I imagine my sister in her gorgeous satin wedding dress, peacock-blue heels peeping out from beneath the hem as she spins around the dance floor in Andrew's arms. A moment that might never happen now, in part thanks to me.

A lump forms in my throat. I've never been someone who gets overly sentimental about weddings — it's always seemed to me like a lot of money to drop on a party — but I suddenly understand why someone might want to have one. While I'm still not totally sold on the idea of happily ever after, I have to admit there is something very romantic about publicly declaring to the world that this is your person, the one that you intend to spend the rest of your life with. And while forever might not actually turn out to be forever for some, maybe it's still worth taking the chance in the end. Maybe love actually is worth the risk.

Halfway through the song, Shep crooks his finger at me, gesturing for me to come over to him.

"Go," Camila says, nudging me in the side as a man in a porkpie hat walks past and throws a toonie into the case. "He wants you to sing with him."

"What?" I shake my head and shrink back against the tiled wall. "He doesn't even know if I can sing!" I mean I can, a little bit, but he doesn't know that!

Besides, does he not remember what happened last night when I gave that horrible speech? He knows that I *hate* being in front of an audience — not that there's much of an audience, hardly anyone is paying attention to him.

I narrow my eyes. Oh, I get it. Shep thinks that singing with him might help cure me of my stage fright. And, okay, logically I know that if I want to get over my fear then I need to just do it, but my feet are rooted to the floor and I can't seem to make them move. Even the thought of standing there with him, drawing attention to myself, makes my hands start to shake.

But Camila makes the decision for me — she grabs my arm and shoves me towards Shep. I stand stiffly by his side, painfully aware of every stranger who so much as glances our way as they walk by, until I look over at Shep. He gives me an encouraging smile and I let out a breath.

Okay, I can do this. *I can do this.*

And so I do. I join him in the chorus, my voice wavering at first. Shep's smile widens and he nods, clearly impressed, so I find the confidence to sing a little stronger, a little louder. And then before I know it, the rest of the world somehow falls away and I forget that people are looking at me. I forget about everything but the two of us staring into each other's eyes and singing this beautiful song, the one my sister and her fiancé were meant to dance to at their wedding tomorrow.

And before I know it, the song is over and we're done. I blink, like I'm coming out of a trance. To my surprise, a group of people have stopped to watch us. My face burns as they clap and whistle, but I'm more proud than embarrassed.

Shep grabs my hand, his warm fingers lacing through mine, and we bow. My nerves start to take over again but being in front of an audience feels a tiny bit less scary than it did before, so I guess that's progress.

"Wow," Camila says, grinning at us as the crowd starts to disburse. "That was amazing! You should sing together more often — your voices really complement each other."

"We definitely should do that again," Shep says to me. "You were incredible, Arden."

He's exaggerating — I'm good but I'm not *that* good — but the fact that he wants to sing with me again makes me glow inside. Not that I think we'll have the chance — I'm leaving in two days, whether the wedding happens or not. That doesn't give us much time for singing or for anything else, unfortunately.

Shep gently squeezes my hand and releases it, then bends down to scoops the coins out of the guitar case.

"Nine dollars," he says. "That'll do." He hands the guitar back to Camila. "Thanks again. You're a lifesaver."

"Don't thank me," she replies. "It was a treat to get to listen to you." She hugs Shep again but his eyes flick to me as he gives her a friendly thump on the back.

"We'd better get going," he says, disentangling himself from her arms.

"Text me. Let's really grab that coffee sometime instead of just talking about it, okay?" Camila says.

Shep nods, but he sneaks another glance at me. "Yeah, sounds good."

Camila turns to me and smiles. "It was nice to meet you Arden," she says. She sounds genuine, which makes me feel like a monster for hoping that she and Shep never have that coffee date — especially when she's just helped us out — but I can't help it.

"Nice to meet you, too," I reply, because it's the polite thing to say and I don't want her to know that I'm burning with jealousy because the reality is she can see him any time she likes — they live in the same city, while I'm a million miles away in San Diego and I might get to hang out with him once a year if I'm lucky.

The high from singing in front of a crowd quickly dims,

replaced with a weary sadness. Camila and Shep make a lot more sense, which is probably why they'll end up together. Even if he wanted to be with me, it wouldn't work out — the distance between us is just too much to ever overcome.

I can tell myself that it doesn't matter all day, but my heart isn't listening. I like him, I can't help it, and it stinks that we'll never have the chance to find out if we could really be something.

Ugh. Feelings suck.

We say goodbye to Camila and hurry over to the fare kiosk to buy another Presto pass, then trace our way back to the bus stop.

"You looked like you were going to pass out when I asked you to sing with me," Shep says, laughing.

I lightly punch his arm. "I felt like I was going to pass out."

"But you didn't," he says. "You did great. I know it's not easy, facing down your fears."

"Yeah, well. Clearly it's something I need to work on." And while I'm not exactly anxious to do it again, maybe it will be a little less terrible next time.

We reach the bus stop. We have a few minutes to kill before the next bus to High Park arrives, so we stand underneath the awning of a nearby building to get some shade.

"You should definitely pursue music," I say to him. "You're so good."

Shep shrugs. "I'd like to try but I'm not sure I'm good enough to make it. My dad's not wrong about the odds of actually being able to earn a living from it."

"Some people do."

"Yeah. I guess that's true."

"You'll never know if you don't try," I say. "Besides, is working in the corporate world really going to make you happy?"

He sighs. "I seriously doubt it."

I seriously doubt it, too, and I've only known him for a day. I can't imagine him doing anything but playing music.

"And you're wrong. You are good enough," I say.

He looks at me, his eyes full of gratitude. "You think so?"

I nod. "I really do." Maybe all he needs is some encouragement. Maybe that's all any of us really need to pursue our dreams.

The bus pulls up. It's already packed with passengers — we probably could have gotten away with getting on without a transit pass, after all — and once again Shep and I have to stand, our arms extended over our heads so we can hang onto the metal pole. Not that I mind because it means that we have to crowd close together, close enough that I'm sure Shep must be able to feel my heart racing.

"Camila's really nice," I say casually as the bus starts to move.

Shep nods. "Yeah, she is."

"I think she's into you." Heat rushes to my face as soon as the words are out of my mouth. Seriously, could I be any more transparent? I might as well just confess that I'm into him. And what am I doing, anyway, digging for information about his feelings for Camila? Do I really want to hear him tell me that he's interested in her? No. No, I do not.

"Nah," Shep says. The bus lurches and his hand moves closer to mine on the bar, sending sparks all the way through me. "We're just friends."

Our eyes meet and I realize that what he's actually

trying to tell me is that I don't need to worry about Camila — she's not the one he's interested in. I smile, but the relief only lasts for about a second, because honestly, if it's not her then it'll just be some other girl. It's never going to be me. Shep and I live thousands of miles apart. It's so not smart to take things to the next level. I know this, but I also know that when it comes right down to it, I'm not going to make the smart decision, I'm going to make the reckless one. I can't help it. I want to know what happens next.

fourteen

TEN MINUTES LATER, Shep and I are standing on the sidewalk across from High Park, which really looks more like an endless expanse of forest than a city park.

"I didn't realize that it was so big," I say, frowning. It's like Balboa Park big. How on earth are we supposed to find Laurel here? If she's even here, that is.

"Yeah, it's like four hundred acres or something, but we're only going to the fountains, it's not like we're checking the entire park," Shep reminds me as he walks over to a row of identical black bicycles lined up in a metal rack. "Let's take the bikes." He slides his phone out of his pocket and opens a bike share app. "It'll be a lot faster than walking, obviously, and we need to make up for lost time."

Right, thanks to my misplaced wallet and the detour to raise enough money for another transit pass we now only have two hours left until the rehearsal dinner. If we don't find my sister within the next half an hour I'm going to have to concede defeat and let Shep call Andrew to tell him that he's been dumped. Just the thought of doing that makes me feel sick to my stomach.

Please God, let Laurel be at the fountains, I pray as Shep unlocks a bike for each of us.

I haven't actually ridden a bicycle in years but apparently it's one of those things that you never forget how to do, so I should be fine.

"Where are the helmets?" I ask as we pull the bikes out of the rack.

"No helmets," he says. "But don't worry, Professor, we'll be really careful. We won't be riding on the street for long, anyway."

My eyebrows rise. If I'm not wearing a helmet and I fall off this bike — which is a strong possibility — my brains will probably end up splattered all over the concrete. And is he seriously telling me that we're going to have to ride on this street with a million cars whizzing by us?

But it seems that he does mean it because he throws his leg over his bicycle and starts to peddle, leaving the sidewalk and entering the bike lane. I swallow and follow after him at a much slower pace, gripping the handlebars so tightly my knuckles turn white.

The hot summer breeze brushes my cheeks as cars rush past way too close for my comfort. Shep checks over his shoulder every so often to make sure that I'm still behind him, slowing down so that I can keep up with him. It's a little thing, but it tells me a lot about him and I wish for the millionth time that we didn't live in completely different countries. It's so unfair.

A few minutes later, Shep extends his arm straight out, signaling that he's about to turn to the right. I relax a little as we pass under a stone and wrought iron arch and into the peaceful shady shelter of the park. We stick snugly to the edge of the wide, gently twisting road, even though only the occasional car passes by us now. The trees are so tall and leafy it's easy to forget that we're even in a city.

I keep an eye out for Laurel as we ride past a playground and a picnic site and the High Park Zoo, hoping that by some miracle I'll spot her. Shep eventually turns right again and slows to a stop near a wide swath of grass.

A sense of desperation settles over me as we park the bikes near a maze of knee-high box hedges. The hedges separate three reflecting pools, each of which has several fountains that are arcing water gracefully into the air. It's beautiful and peaceful and I can see why my sister likes to come here.

We walk onto the path. People are milling about, taking photos, couples walking hand in hand, parents wrangling their kids. There's a big part of me that wants to freeze this moment in time or, better yet, to get back on my bike and just keep riding forever, so that I don't have to face what will happen if we don't find my sister.

I wipe my sweaty hands on my dress as we walk down a few steps. I scan the gardens, but Laurel isn't here. *Of course she isn't here*, I think, my chin starting to quiver. Why did I ever think that I'd be able to find her in a city of this size? And why — *why* — did Laurel take what I said in my speech last night to heart? I'm the last person she should ever listen to on matters of the heart. I don't know *anything* about love. I've never even had a serious boyfriend!

Shep lets out a weary sigh and rubs his hand over his

face. "Well, I guess that's it, then. We've checked every place on our list."

He's right — there's nowhere left to look. It's over. Time to give up.

Tears sting my eyes. I turn away from Shep so that he won't see I'm trying not to cry, but I guess I'm not doing a very good job of hiding it because he's suddenly in front of me.

"Hey, it's going to be alright," he says, sliding his arms around me. I lean my forehead on his chest. "Whatever happens now, we'll deal with it. It'll be okay, Arden."

I don't know how he can say that — it doesn't feel like anything is going to be okay ever again. How am I ever going to face Andrew, after what I've done? I wouldn't blame him if he hates me forever for what I did. I know I hate me at the moment. If I'd just written a speech like Laurel asked me to, something sweet and thoughtful, then this never would have happened. Sure, Kaito and my dad both bear some responsibility, too, but this is mostly on me. I know it.

I let myself cry — for Laurel, for me, but most of all for Andrew and the pain he's about to experience. I can't imagine how hurt and humiliated he's going to feel when he finds out what Laurel has done. And I can't bear how awful it's going to be for Shep to have to tell him.

Shep's arms tighten around me. When I finally calm down, I let out a long, shuddering breath and disentangle myself from his arms, embarrassed that I just bawled all over the front of his t-shirt.

"This sucks," I say, wiping my eyes.

"Yeah, it does."

"I just feel so bad for your brother."

He nods. "Me too. But I'd feel a lot worse if Laurel had doubts and married him anyway. And once some time has passed, Andrew will realize that too."

I grimace. "Yeah, well, she probably wouldn't have had those doubts if I hadn't given that stupid speech."

"It's not your fault, Arden," he says. "There's no way that your speech would have caused Laurel to cancel the wedding unless she was already thinking about doing it."

He's just being nice and trying to let me off the hook, but there's no excuse — I'm sure that my sister wouldn't have taken off like this if I hadn't blathered on about the odds of her marriage failing.

And at this point, I may not even get the chance to talk to her before my mom and I leave on Monday — who knows when she'll come out of hiding.

"I guess I'd better call Andrew," Shep says, although he looks like he'd rather eat glass than actually do that. "No use putting this off any longer."

"You can't tell him over the phone," I say. Andrew deserves to hear this news directly, and since Laurel was too chicken to do it, it's up to Shep to break it to him in as kind a way as possible.

"You're right," he agrees. "I'll head over to their apartment as soon as I take you back to your hotel."

"Don't worry about me," I say. "I can figure out how to get back on my own." I hope so, anyway. It won't be a super straightforward route, considering that I have to make a stop at the art gallery to pick up my wallet first.

"Besides, there's less than two hours left until the rehearsal dinner," I add. "It's way more important that you talk to Andrew." The only thing that could make this day any worse is if he showed up at the restaurant, unaware that his wedding has been called off.

Shep shakes his head. "We've already lost one Stewart sister in this city today, I'm going to make sure that we don't lose another," he says. "Besides, it should only take me about forty-five minutes to take you to the hotel and then get over to his place. Andrew and I are supposed to go to the rehearsal dinner together, anyway, so he'll be expecting me."

"Okay," I say. Selfishly, I'm relieved. Not only because it'll be much less stressful navigating the city if he's still around to guide me, but also because this might be the last bit of time that we get to spend together — once word gets out that the wedding is off and Shep's family circles around him I might not have the opportunity to see him again. At least not on this trip. And maybe not ever, if Andrew decides he wants to cut all ties with our family. And how could he not want to? Who wants to keep in touch with the girl who ruined your life?

It's not until Shep and I are about to leave the garden that I remember that the reason we included the fountains on our list in the first place — this is where Laurel and Andrew got engaged. It's like a punch to the heart, remembering how thrilled she was when he asked her to marry him and something about being in the same place as the two of them were on that momentous occasion makes me even sadder.

And just because I like to punish myself, I pull out my phone and open Instagram. I scroll through my sister's feed and, sure enough, there's their engagement photo — Laurel and Andrew standing in front of one of the fountains in their puffy winter jackets and matching black beanies, snowflakes falling all around them. My sister is beaming at her brand-new fiancé, her hand extended towards the camera to show off the sparkling diamond ring on her finger.

"Look," I say, tipping the phone towards Shep to show him the photo as we head up the path. "They were so happy!"

"Yeah, they were," Shep says. "I never would have guessed this is where they'd end up."

Me neither.

"Did they ever tell you the story of how they got engaged?" I ask him.

Shep nods. "I knew that Andrew had been wanting to ask her for a while," he says. "He knew that Laurel loved the holidays, so he decided to do it at the outdoor rink here in the park, but when they got there, there were so many people skating that he changed his mind. He didn't want to ask her in front of anyone."

"So he took her for a walk instead," my voice thick as I pick up the story. "Laurel thought it was strange because it was December and well below freezing and your brother hates the cold."

"That should have been a dead giveaway," Shep says.

"Laurel said her fingers were almost frostbitten by the time they got to the fountains, even though she was wearing gloves," I add.

Shep snort-laughs. "It didn't occur to my brother that the fountains weren't even on in the winter until they got here. There wasn't anything to see but snow."

"That didn't matter to Laurel," I say. "All that mattered

was Andrew. She said that she was stunned when he dropped to one knee and asked her to marry him."

"He told me the right leg of his jeans were soaking wet the entire ride home," Shep says. "But he was way too happy to care."

Andrew and Laurel had such a romantic start that it's hard to believe this is how it ends for them. I may not totally believe in happily ever after, but my sister does — or she did, anyway.

I feel tears threaten again. I swallow and glance at the caption Laurel included underneath their engagement photo that they asked a passing stranger to take of them:

How could I say no?

My stomach drops. How could she say no? That doesn't sound like someone who is off-the-charts excited to be marrying the love of her life — it sounds like someone who felt like she didn't have any other choice.

I blink, wondering if I'm reading too much into this. It's just a caption, she probably didn't even think twice about it. Maybe I'm wrong — maybe I'm overreacting.

Except if I'm not, then Laurel's decision not to go through with the wedding has nothing to do with me and everything to do with the fact that she just doesn't want to get married.

This should probably make me feel better — if I'm right about this photo, then it doesn't matter what I said in my speech last night and I have nothing to feel guilty about. It's not my fault that my sister took off.

"What?" Shep asks, noticing that I've stiffened up. I point to the caption, wondering if he'll come to the same conclusion that I have.

"Yikes," he says, frowning. "How did we all miss that?"

I shake my head. "We missed it because Laurel seemed so happy and excited."

His face hardens. "I don't get it," he says. "Why would she accept my brother's proposal if she wasn't feeling it? And why would she let it get this far if she didn't want to marry him?"

"Because she loves him," I say. Laurel might have been conflicted about getting married, but I know that she loves Andrew — she never would have said yes to him otherwise. Maybe she hoped that she'd be ready by the time the wedding rolled around, that she could go through with it for him.

"If she loved him she wouldn't have dumped him," Shep says. "And she definitely wouldn't have just left him a note."

I mean, it's hard to argue with that. Breaking up with someone via a note is a dick move, totally inexcusable, and I'm disappointed in Laurel for messing everything up, but I also feel like I have to defend her — she is my sister, after all. "I think she's just really freaked out," I say. "She probably didn't know how to tell him and this seemed like the easiest way."

"For her, maybe," Shep says. "Not for my brother." He shakes his head with disgust and stalks towards the bikes. I slide my phone back into my bag and follow after him, full of secondhand shame.

He's silent as we ride through the park, silent as we return the bikes to the rack and wait for the bus, silent on the bus ride back to the art gallery.

I'm quiet, too, because I don't know what to say that would make any of this better — probably because there is nothing to say that could make it better. Anger is rolling off Shep in waves, but I understand it — if I found out that Andrew had been having doubts about marrying my sister for months but waited until the day before their wedding to walk out on her I would be furious too. I would also be upset if I was stuck having to tell her that she'd been dumped because her fiancé was too chicken to do it.

I glance over at Shep. He's staring out the bus window, his face tense. I swallow and reach for his hand, my heart pounding. I want him to know that I'm here and that I'm sorry that I couldn't fix this.

He glances down at our entwined fingers and then over at me and his expression softens a little. He gives me a small smile before turning to look out the window again, but he doesn't let go of my hand.

fifteen

HALF AN HOUR LATER, I run inside the gift shop at the AGO to grab my wallet and then Shep and I rush to St. Patrick's station to catch the next train. I am dreading going back to the hotel. My mom is going to lose her mind when she finds out that I've been lying to her all day about Laurel, but there's no getting around it now — I have to tell her.

On the way to the escalator, we pass by a busker — an older man with blonde dreadlocks butchering a Bruce Springsteen song — and Shep throws the rest of the change we earned from our (much better) performance into the man's guitar case.

As we wait on the subway platform, the air hot and stuffy and smelling strongly of body odor, I grow more and more uncomfortable that Shep and I still aren't talking. Finally, I can't stand it anymore.

"So there was this demigod named Sciron," I say. It's the first myth that comes to mind, one of a hundred that I'm able to pull out of my brain at any time, like some kind of odd party trick. I glance over at Shep to see if he's open to me continuing with the story of if he'd rather I just shut up and give him some peace.

He looks at me and asks, "What exactly is a demigod?"

"Part-human, part-God," I say, relaxing a little. "Anyway, Sciron was a bandit and he was all about robbing people. He'd wait for travelers to come by on the road and then he'd steal everything they had and force them to wash his feet—"

Shep narrows his eyes. "He forced people to wash his feet?"

I nod. "And that's not even the most screwed up part," I say. "Once they knelt down, he'd kick them off the cliff and into the sea."

"So he wasn't just a bandit, he was also a psycho serial killer."

"Yes," I say. "Although sometimes the fall didn't kill these people, so it was up to the big tortoise waiting at the bottom to finish them off."

Shep's mouth twitches with a smile. "Are you saying that a turtle was his accomplice?"

"Apparently." I smile back at him, relieved that my story seems to be taking his mind off the fact that he's going to have to tell his brother that he's been left at the altar. "Sciron killed a lot of people this way, but finally, Theseus —"

"The guy who killed the minotaur and then ditched his girlfriend on the island to starve to death?"

"That's him," I say. "Well, Theseus caught wind of what was happening and he didn't like it at all, so he tracked Sciron down and tossed him off a cliff."

"Poetic justice," Shep says. "The dude got what he deserved."

"Oh, he totally did."

After a minute, he adds, "It's interesting. Theseus was the hero when he killed the minotaur, but a villain when he ghosted his girlfriend, and in this myth he's the hero again. So which is he, really?"

I shrug. "I think he's both," I say. "I mean, if you think about it, we're probably all villains in someone else's story." My sister, for example, isn't going to come out of this situation looking very good, but that doesn't mean that she's a terrible person — she just handled things very badly. I hope Andrew and his family will eventually be able to understand that and won't hate her forever.

The subway pulls into the station and Shep and I get on board. The train's a lot less crowded than it was earlier in the day and we easily find two seats together.

"It should only take us about fifteen minutes or so to get to the hotel," Shep says as I settle in beside him.

My heart sinks. Once he drops me off who knows when — or if — I'll ever see him again. The thought depresses me.

I sigh and glance out the window, but we're deep underground so there isn't anything to see except darkness. We haven't been on the train long when it starts to slow down. I assume it's because we're approaching the next station, but then the lights flicker and we roll to a stop in the middle of the tunnel. A collective groan goes up from the other passengers.

"What's going on?" I ask Shep. "Why are we stopped?"

He grimaces. "It happens sometimes. Hopefully we won't be stuck here for long."

My breathing starts to quicken. We're stuck? It's one thing to be inside a train that's moving through a tunnel far below the earth, it's quite another to be at a stand-still, with no way to get out.

"What's the longest amount of time you've been stopped for?" I ask him, feeling queasy.

"Forty-five minutes," he replies.

My eyes widen. Forty-five minutes? But we don't have forty-five minutes to spare! I might not be super anxious to get back to the hotel and inform my mom that the wedding is off and that Laurel is missing, but Shep needs to get to Andrew as soon as possible. We're already cutting it way too close to the rehearsal dinner.

"I'm sure we'll start moving again before long," Shep reassures me, but I can tell that he's worried, too. He pulls out his phone and frowns. "Great. No service."

I try my phone but I have no bars either. This is a disaster! We're completely cut off from the world down here, with no way to even call Andrew if we had to. Not only that, but the air conditioning seems to be off and it's miserably, horribly, disgustingly hot on this train. I take my water out of my bag and down the rest of the bottle in one long gulp.

The intercom crackles. "Good afternoon, everyone," a man says. "Looks like there's an issue on the track ahead. Please sit tight and we'll get going again as soon as possible."

"What are some of the reasons that trains stop?" I ask Shep.

"Could be anything — there might be a problem with the train ahead, like sometimes the doors get stuck, or there's a medical emergency or some idiot isn't behaving themselves and has to be removed," he says. "Or maybe there's someone on the track."

My stomach lurches at the idea that we're stopped because someone might have jumped in front of the train. I might like dark stories, but that's just because their fictional — it's the real-life stuff that scares me.

"I'm sure that's not it, though," Shep says hurriedly, noticing my freaked-out expression. He reaches over and lightly squeezes my hand. "How about another one of your myths, Professor? Something really twisted and weird. I could use the distraction."

I know that he's only asking me to do this in the hopes that it will divert my attention from the fact that we're stuck far underground, but it works — I start to mentally file through every myth I know, trying to decide which one to tell him.

"Okay, so there was this guy named Ixion who had been exiled for a bunch of crimes," I say. "I don't know why, exactly, but I guess he must have been a pretty bad dude. For some reason, Zeus — who wasn't the most noble guy either — decided that it would be a good idea to invite Ixion to Mount Olympus." I shift in my seat, aware that my bare leg is now resting against his bare leg. I flush, but I don't move away.

"Mount Olympus is a real place, isn't it?" Shep asks.

"Yes, it's the highest mountain in Greece. You can actually climb it, which I would totally love to do one day," I reply. "Anyway, Ixion happily takes Zeus up on his offer because he's sick and tired of being stuck in exile, but when he arrives on Olympus, he starts to get a little too friendly with Zeus's wife, Hera."

I look over at Shep, my stomach flipping when I see that he's staring intently at me. "Zeus quickly realized that his new friend was hot for his wife, but instead of telling him to take a hike, he decided to test his loyalty — he wanted to know if Ixion would actually betray him by acting on those feelings. So he created a cloud that looked exactly like Hera. And Ixion totally fell for it. He hooked up with the cloud and got it pregnant—"

"Excuse me, what?" Shep asks, starting to laugh.

I smile. "Well, as you can imagine, Zeus wasn't very happy that Ixion failed his little test, so he turned him into a giant flaming wheel."

"Of course he did. How else was he supposed to respond?"

I laugh. "The cloud ended up giving birth to Centaurus, who then grew up and had sex with a bunch of horses, thereby creating centaurs."

"That makes total sense," Shep says.

I grin at him. "Hey, you asked for twisted and weird."

"You're right. I did ask for that." He grins back at me and my heart skips. "You really do know your Greek mythology."

"For all you know, I could just be making all of this up," I say with a straight face.

Shep bumps my shoulder with his own. "If you were able to make up a story on the spot about a guy who got a cloud pregnant then I'm definitely impressed." He holds my gaze for a moment, trying to decide whether or not I'm bluffing.

I cave. "Fine, I can't take the credit. I didn't make it up."

"I'm still impressed," he replies in a much softer voice. He's looking at me closely, his eyes tracing my face, and I'm pretty sure that he's trying to work up the nerve to kiss me. My pulse starts to race. I want to kiss him, too — very badly — but I don't want to do it here, trapped on a train in a dark tunnel, surrounded by bunch of strangers.

I glance away from him and the moment is lost — and I instantly regret it. Time is not on our side — there aren't going to be a million chances for us to make out. Depending on what happens after Shep delivers me back to the hotel, I might never see him again.

Shep clears his throat. "So what are you going to do for the rest of the summer?"

"Nothing much," I reply. There's still a few more weeks until senior year starts, but I'll be spending it working at the ice cream shack and hanging out with my friends back home. In other words, nothing exciting.

"Yeah, me either," Shep says. "I'll just be killing time until September."

"Are you excited to be going to York? I hear it's a good school."

"It is. I was lucky to get in."

"Do they have a music program?" I ask.

He smiles. "They do. And I know where you're going with this, but I'd have to audition."

"Then you should totally audition."

"It's too late for this semester," he says. "If I do decide to pursue music seriously, I'd probably try to get into U of T. They have one of the best music programs in the country."

"U of T?"

"University of Toronto."

"Oh. Right."

He gets quiet again, clearly thinking about something.

All around us, people are getting restless as they wait for the train to start moving. A mother is walking a sobbing baby up and down the aisle while a group of boys a little younger than us are trying to see who can hold a chin-up for the longest on the metal bars near the ceiling. An older man decked out in running shorts and a Toronto Blue Jays t-shirt keeps sighing loudly and looking at his watch.

Shep shifts in his seat so that he's facing me. "You know, I'm super pissed at Laurel for doing this to my brother, but I guess I can sort of understand why she might not want to get married," he says. "She did tell me that your parents had a pretty nasty divorce."

"That's putting it lightly," I reply. "They can't stand each other. I'm surprised they managed to get through dinner last night without an argument." It's definitely a first.

"They still fight even though they aren't together anymore?"

I nod. "Pretty much whenever they're in the same room together, which luckily isn't very often." It's usually my mom who starts it, but it doesn't take much to draw my dad into a fight — she knows exactly what buttons to push with him.

Shep frowns. "That must be awful for you."

I shrug but honestly it is awful and I resent both of them for it. They don't need to be best friends but I wish that they could put their differences aside and just get along for Laurel and me. It's pretty much the least they could do.

"Do you ever wonder how it all went so wrong between them?" he asks, his brow furrowing. "I mean, they must have loved each other when they got married, so what happened to push them so far apart?"

"I don't think it was just one thing," I say. My parents got married young, they hadn't been together long enough to really know each other and they were opposites in pretty much every way — it would have been surprising if it did work, I guess. I can't even pinpoint the moment their marriage went south because as far back as I can remember they weren't happy together. It was classic lets-stay-together-for-the-kids, but it ended up doing more harm than good.

"We're all happier now that they're divorced," I add.

"My parents are still sickeningly into each other," Shep says. "It can be kind of embarrassing sometimes."

I know I'm supposed to be grossed out by the idea of his parents showing affection, but there's something really sweet — and reassuring — about the idea that two people who have been together for ages can still be madly in love with each other. It gives me some hope.

Shep glances at his phone. "Still no service," he says, chewing his bottom lip. "It's been almost twenty minutes since we stopped."

I swallow, feeling helpless. This is out of our hands — there's nothing we can do but wait and I hate waiting, especially when there is so much at stake. We can't let Andrew show up to the rehearsal dinner — I can't bear the thought of him finding out that Laurel has left him in front of all his family and friends.

"We need a backup plan," I say.

"Like what? Break open the doors and run down the tracks?" Shep replies.

"I was thinking more along the lines of asking if

someone on here has service and if so can we borrow their phone."

He huffs a laugh. "Yeah, that sounds like a better idea."

I lean across the aisle, about to ask the woman sitting across from us if her cell phone is working when the train finally starts to move again. A cheer goes up and I let out a relieved breath and sink back into my seat.

"Thank the Greek gods," Shep says.

sixteen

"WE'RE RIGHT in the middle of the U of T campus," Shep says five minutes later as we leave the subway station. "If we'd gone through the other exit we'd be right across the street from The Faculty of Music."

I'm about to nudge him towards auditioning for the music program again — clearly he's dying to try out and just needs a little push to actually do it — when my phone starts to blow up. I take it out of my bag, my eyes widening when I see that I have sixteen missed calls and messages.

My first thought is that Laurel has finally gotten back to me, but once again, I'm disappointed — none of the messages are from her. A couple are from my dad and Riya, but most of them are from my mom, which in itself isn't that strange — she spams me all the time.

I open Riya's text first, figuring that she's just checking in or giving me an update on their shopping trip, maybe letting me know what time they're planning on heading back to the hotel, but unfortunately, that's not the case.

RIYA: Your mom's in Laurel's room — I couldn't stop

her, I'm sorry . She knows L is missing. You'd better get back here asap!

My stomach drops all the way down to my toes. My fingers are shaking as I open the string of messages from my mother, cringing as I see that she's yelling at me over text.

ARDEN STEWART WHAT IS GOING ON?

WHERE IS YOUR SISTER??

WHERE ARE YOU?

WHY AREN'T YOU ANSWERING YOUR PHONE??

CALL ME!!!

Oh crap. I'm in so much trouble.

I stop walking. Shep continues on, still talking about the music program, before he realizes that I'm not beside him. He stops and turns around to look at me.

"Arden?" he asks. "What's wrong?"

"My mom knows that Laurel's missing."

Shep grimaces. "Well, that's not good."

Understatement. My mom can be pretty unpredictable, so I'm worried that she'll decide to pick up the phone and call Andrew to grill him about what's going on before Shep has a chance to get to him.

I feel sick.

"You'd better get over to Andrew and Laurel's apartment right away," I say to him. "I can find my way back to the hotel on my own."

Shep nods and rubs his jaw, his face tight with stress. "We're only a few blocks away. You just need to head directly up this street and turn right on Yorkville."

I nod. Sounds easy enough.

Neither of us move. Instead, we stand on the sidewalk and stare at each other — this is the moment that I've been dreading, the moment when we have to say goodbye and go our separate ways, possibly forever.

The way Shep is looking at me is making my heart race. He walks over, closing the distance between us.

"I know I probably shouldn't say this, considering the circumstances," he says. "But I had a lot of fun hanging out with you today."

"I had a lot of fun with you, too." He's standing close enough that if I just moved forward an inch or two I'd be in his arms. "Thanks for coming with me," I add. "I wouldn't have gotten this far without you." We may not have found my sister, but I'm grateful that at least we tried — it makes me feel a tiny less guilty for my role in all of this.

Shep smiles sadly. "I was really hoping this day would end differently."

"Me too." I really thought we'd be able to fix this. I was so sure that Laurel would change her mind and that Shep and I would be hanging out at her wedding tomorrow.

He nods and his eyes flick to my lips. I'm almost positive that he's going to kiss me, but instead he takes another step forward and gives me a bear hug, his arms wrapping tightly around me. I put my arms around him, too, and rest my cheek on his chest, breathing in the clean, cottony smell of him, trying to memorize everything about this moment.

What would have happened between us if we'd had more time together? Maybe nothing. Or maybe everything. Either way, I guess I'll never know now.

I close my eyes. This is like my own personal Greek tragedy.

"Bye Arden," Shep whispers into my hair. I shiver, even though it's like a million degrees outside.

"Bye Shep," I whisper back.

He gives me a final squeeze and walks away.

This is for the best, I think as I watch him head back towards the subway station. If we'd spent the rest of the weekend together then it would be even harder to leave him on Monday, harder to move on with my life afterwards. It's better that we didn't take that next step.

That's what I tell myself, anyway.

Just before he heads inside the station, Shep turns around again to look at me. "Text me when you get to the hotel, okay Professor?" he says. "Just so I know that you made it back there safely."

"Okay," I say, my throat thick. It's broad daylight and his directions are so straightforward that even I can't mess them up, but it's sweet that he's worried about me. There are so many things that I like about him, I'm not sure how any other guy is ever going to measure up. Shep Tremblay is probably going to haunt me for a very long time.

He waves and then disappears into the station and I let out a heavy sigh, wondering if that's the last time that I'll ever see him. It's too depressing to think about, so as I'm walking towards the hotel, I distract myself by sending Riya a text to let her know that I'm on the way. And then I click on the message from my dad.

Your mother's on a rampage. Heading to your hotel to try and calm her down.

My stomach drops. Why on earth would my dad think that he'd be able to calm my mother down? Have the millions of arguments they've had over the years taught him nothing? He's just going to make everything worse. Much, much worse!

I check the time stamp on his message — he sent it half an hour ago when I was trapped on the subway, which means that he's probably already close to my hotel by now. I start to walk even faster, firing a text back to him:

DAD! Please don't go to the hotel!!!!! I'm on my way and will handle Mom!!!!! Do. Not. Go. To. The. Hotel!!!!

As I'm typing, my phone vibrates with another message from Riya:

Hurry! Your dad is here and all hell is breaking loose!

Oh my god.

I start to run, dodging people on the sidewalks, my bag thumping painfully against my hip. By the time I reach The Hazelton five minutes later, I'm soaked with sweat and sucking in big gulps of air. I dash across the lobby and over to the bank of elevators, punching the button a few times, even though logically I know that's not going to bring an elevator down any faster.

I pace back and forth, then press the elevator button a few more times.

Come on, come on, come on!

I catch a glimpse of myself in the large gilt-edged mirror hanging at the end of the hall and flinch. I look like a hot mess. My face is bright red and my hair is frizzy and doing it's best to escape from my ponytail. My dress has big dark stains under the armpits. I actually have pit stains! God, I really hope that happened on the run over here and not while I was with Shep.

I'm all slouchy, too, and I can hear my mom's voice

ringing in my ears, nagging me about my posture and instructing me to stand up straight. I pull my shoulders back and adjust my bag on my shoulder, which is when I remember that I still have Laurel's note to Andrew, as well as her engagement ring and the gift he bought for her. I chew my lip. I should have given all of it to Shep so he could pass them on to his brother.

Then again, maybe it's not so terrible that I still have these things — I'll have to return them before I leave town. My heart lifts a little. Maybe I will have the chance to see Shep again after all.

I'm in the middle of texting him to let him know that I have this stuff and that I'm back at the hotel as the elevator doors on the far right slide open. I walk inside and hit the button for the eighth floor, still typing as a few more people get on.

"Hi Arden," a voice says, as a hairy hand reaches past me and pushes the button for the fourth floor.

I glance up from my phone to see Charlotte and Nathalie, each holding several large shopping bags, along with the owner of the hand, a man in a pale grey business suit who immediately moves away from us to the back of the elevator.

"Wow, are you okay?" Charlotte's forehead wrinkles in concern as she reaches out to touch my arm. "You look like you're about to pass out."

"And you're all sweaty," Nathalie says, wrinkling her nose in such a way that makes me think that pit stains aren't my only problem.

"I'm okay," I say.

I'm totally not okay. I will probably never be okay again.

"What did the doctor say?" Charlotte asks me. "Was she able to help Laurel?"

I swallow. I should probably tell them what's happening — they're going to find out soon enough anyway — but I guess there's still a part of me that's hoping that my sister will turn up and this nightmare will be over. "She's still not a hundred percent," I say.

I feel bad lying to Charlotte. Not so much to Nathalie, who I still haven't quite forgiven for calling me out about my speech in front of everyone at lunch. Also she basically just said I smell, so.

"Oh no. She's not going to miss the rehearsal dinner is she?" Charlotte frowns as the elevator slows at the fourth floor and the man gets off. "That would be really awful."

Not as awful as missing her actual wedding.

"There's no way that Laurel's going to skip her rehearsal dinner," Nathalie says, as the doors close and we start to move again. "She'll drag herself to the restaurant even if she still has a migraine."

Oh how I wish that were true.

But I just shrug because I don't know what to say. I hope that Laurel will be able to lean on them when the truth comes out. My sister might be the one making the decision to call off the wedding, but I know that this isn't easy for her and she's probably feeling pretty devastated right now. She's really going to need her friends.

Nathalie studies a chip in her hot pink manicure. "What time are we getting our nails done tomorrow?"

"Nine o'clock," I say, my chest tightening. We have a group appointment at the hotel spa tomorrow morning to get glam for the wedding. I wonder if I should cancel the appointments or if it's super insensitive to just keep them and get a massage. After the day I've had, I could certainly use one.

The elevator slows again as it arrives at our floor. The doors open and the three of us step into the hall.

"Are you sure you're okay?" Charlotte asks me again.

"I'm fine."

"You should try and get some rest before dinner. Maybe take a nap."

"I think I will," I say.

I totally won't. I'm going to be too busy trying to keep my mother from spontaneously combusting.

"I guess we'll see you downstairs in an hour," Charlotte adds.

I nod, deciding to let Riya deal with updating them. Maybe they can all go to the restaurant anyway — Laurel had the place closed specifically for the rehearsal dinner, so there will be plenty of food. Someone might as well enjoy it.

We head in opposite directions, Charlotte and Nathalie to their shared room and me to Laurel's. As I walk further down the hall, the sound of my parents screaming at each other from inside my sister's suite reaches my ears.

"...I am not going to let you pin this on me, Sheryl! I've barely seen Laurel since we arrived, no thanks to you. How do you think Rachel and I felt at dinner last night, having to sit all the way at the end of the table—"

"Oh no, I am not going to let you turn this around on me! It's not my fault that you don't have a great relationship with your daughter! You're the one who...."

I stand in front of the door and close my eyes, my

stomach tight with nerves. I was expecting to walk into a scene, but this is next level, even for them.

I really, *really* don't want to go in there. I think about turning around and leaving, going back to my own room and letting them tire themselves out, but it's not fair to let Riya deal with my parents — they're not her problem, they're mine.

And so I take a deep breath and open the door. Riya is standing just on the other side and she looks shell-shocked.

"Thank god you're here," she says. "I was afraid they'd kill each other if I left them alone."

I shake my head. I'm so embarrassed that she's been drawn into this situation. I know how close she and Laurel are, so I assume that she's heard plenty about my parents toxic relationship over the years, but hearing about it is very different than actually witnessing it firsthand. It still rattles me, even though I've seen them like this more times than I can count.

My parents are facing off on either side of Laurel's bed and they're so busy arguing that they haven't even regis-tered that I'm in the room. My dad's face is bright red and my mom is standing with her arms crossed, mascara tracks on her cheeks. She's still wearing the feathered hat she had on at lunch and I notice that she's dropped a shopping bag from Laurel's favorite store, Aritzia, on the desk — she must have come to the room because she bought my sister something.

"*— poisoning her against me for years —*"

"*— not going to let you gaslight me anymore, Kevin —*"

"*— you knew exactly what you were doing —*"

"STOP!" I shout. For once, I'm much louder than they are

and it shocks them into silence. My dad immediately looks contrite but my mom quickly recovers and redirects her anger towards me.

"Arden, where have you been?" she says, narrowing her eyes at me. "I am *furious* that didn't tell me about Laurel. You should have come to me the minute you discovered that she was gone."

"I didn't want to worry you," I say. *And I knew you'd flip out.* "I was hoping that I'd find her and everything would be fine."

"Lay off her, Sheryl," my dad says. "This isn't Arden's fault."

My mom whips around to tell him off and here they go again, arguing and tossing the blame around. I'm relieved that Riya slipped out of the room because I'm about to totally lose it on my parents.

"WILL YOU BOTH JUST SHUT UP!" I'm so angry that I'm shaking. I'm tired of trying to mediate between them. They've been so wrapped up in one-upping each other all these years that they can't see the effect their vitriol has had on my sister and me.

"You want to know why Laurel ran away?" I yell at them. "It's because she was afraid that if she got married then she and Andrew would end up like the two of you!"

"That's not true—" my mom starts to say.

"It is true," I cut her off. "You can't even get along for one day! One stupid day! This is all your fault." Sure, I may have set Laurel off with my speech last night, but that was just the final straw. The real problem is my parents. It's always been my parents.

Well, I can't take it anymore. I can't take them anymore.

And so, before either of them can say another word or try and comfort me, I stomp out of the room, slamming the door on my way out.

Let them do their worst to each other. I'm done with trying to mediate between them.

seventeen

THIS HAS TRULY BEEN the worst day ever.

I storm down the hall and take the elevator to the lobby, not really sure where I'm going, I just know that I want to get as far away from my parents as possible. I'm dying to lie down, pull the covers over my head and bawl my eyes out, but I can't go back to my room — I'm sharing with my mom and obviously that will be the first place she'll look for me.

I keep my head down as I speed walk through the lobby, praying that I won't run into anyone from the wedding party because I'm in no mood to talk. I manage to find a quiet corner tucked away from the main area where I'm hoping my parents won't find me. I sink down into a green velvet wing chair, drop my bag at my feet and let out a long, weary breath. I'm exhausted. This is the first time this entire day that I haven't been in a rush to get somewhere.

I might never move from this spot.

I lean my head against the back of the chair. Now that my mom knows that Laurel's cancelled the wedding it's only a matter of time before the rest of the world finds out, too. My sister is about to become the center of attention in a way that none of us expected. This weekend was supposed to be about uniting two people and their families together but instead it's going to split us all apart.

I close my eyes, wondering what's going to happen now. I'm almost certain that when Laurel finally turns up my mom will try and convince her to come back to San Diego with us. I would be so happy if my sister moved home — maybe then we could begin to repair our relationship — but I can't see her agreeing to that. She's built a life here and while that life may not be going according to plan at the moment, I know that she loves Toronto and her friends and her job. Despite everything that's happened today, I can't imagine that she'll want to leave this city.

I'm sure that she'll let Andrew have their place — she can't dump him the day before their wedding and take their apartment, too — which means that she'll have to find somewhere else to live. School doesn't start for another few weeks, maybe I can talk my mom into letting me stay and help Laurel through this. Maybe that's the silver lining in this whole situation — I can be there for my sister in a way that I haven't been in a long, long time.

I open my eyes and reach for my purse, intending to pull out my phone and text Laurel to let her know that I'm on her side and that I'll help her through this. But as I'm digging through my bag, I notice the gift that Shep brought over for her this morning. The light blue wrapping paper is wrinkled and one corner is torn, having spent all day tumbling around with the rest of my stuff. I stare at the present for a minute, knowing that I should leave it alone, but curiosity gets the better of me and before I can stop myself I'm unwrapping it. Laurel's not going to keep whatever this is anyway and one day she might want to know what Andrew bought her.

I rip the paper off, revealing a small square box printed with cartoon sushi rolls. I frown. Weird choice but I guess it must be an inside joke or something.

I open the box. He's given her a beautiful silver envelope-shaped locket. I pry the locket open and slide out a tiny letter engraved with their wedding date and one word: Forever.

A wave of sadness washes over me as I snap the box shut, intending to put the necklace back in my purse for safekeeping until I can give it back to Andrew, when I glance at the sushi rolls again and something tickles at the edge of my memory.

Laurel and Andrew went for sushi on their first date.

My heart starts to kick up speed. I remember Laurel calling me a few years ago to tell me that she'd met an amazing guy and they'd spent hours at a restaurant gorging on salmon sashimi and getting tipsy on sake until the place closed down for the night.

I think I know where my sister is.

My hands are shaking as I grab my phone to Facetime Shep, ignoring a million texts from my parents. I have to stop him from talking to Andrew. The phone rings twice before he picks up. My heart skips when his face fills the screen.

"Hey," he says.

"Where are you?" I ask him. *Please don't be at the apartment yet.*

"I just got off the train." He turns the phone around to

show me the path we walked on earlier through Trinity Bell-woods park. "Almost at Andrew and Laurel's place."

My shoulders relax a little. There's still time to make this right. "Okay, well, I need you to hold off going there for now," I say.

Shep's brow furrows. "What? Why?"

"Because I'm pretty sure I know where Laurel is."

He shakes his head. "We've already looked all over the city for her," he says. "It's time to give up, Arden. We can't keep this from my brother any longer — we're supposed to leave for the rehearsal dinner soon."

"I know, I know, but *please* just give me another half an hour," I beg. I tell him about the sushi box and Andrew and Laurel's first date, how my sister claimed that she knew from that very first night that his brother was the one for her.

"Well, she seems to have changed her mind about that," he points out, frowning at me. But to my relief, he stops walking and plunks down on a park bench.

"I'm not so sure about that," I reply. If Laurel is actually at the restaurant, the place where it all began, then I think it could mean that she's still in love with Andrew. Maybe it's her way of trying to be close to him.

"Look, I know that what Laurel did is unforgivable and I know that it's asking a lot but please give me one last chance to find her," I say.

Shep makes a face but I can see that he's torn. Deep down, he must think there's still hope for them, too, because he sighs heavily and says, "How long is it going to take you to get from your hotel to the restaurant?"

I wince. "Okay, so there is one tiny problem," I say. "I

don't actually remember the name of the restaurant. I was hoping that you'd know."

"No idea," he says and my heart sinks. "I've never even thought to ask what the two of them did on their first date." He chews his lower lip. "Arden, if we don't know the name of the place then I'm not sure how you're ever going to find it — there's, like, a billion sushi restaurants in the city."

I definitely don't have time to check a billion restaurants. I barely have time to check one — the rehearsal dinner is in less than an hour.

"Maybe you could ask your brother," I suggest.

"How am I supposed to do that?" Shep says. "Hey, bro, just wondering, totally out of the blue, if you can tell me the name of the place where you and Laurel went for your first date?" He shakes his head. "He's not an idiot. He's going to know that something's up."

"I guess I could ask Riya...or wait a minute!"

Laurel posted a photo of their first date on Instagram — I remember looking at it after she called me to tell me about Andrew. I open the app and quickly scroll through her photos, all the way back through the years until I find it — the two of them sitting close together in a booth, Laurel in a little black dress, Andrew beaming at her, clearly already smitten.

The caption reads "our place" and she included a California roll emoji. Fortunately, she also tagged the location.

"Aijou," I say, triumphantly. I quickly google the address. "It's near the Distillery district. Isn't that the same area where the rehearsal dinner is being held?"

"Yes," Shep says. "But it's going to take you at least twenty minutes to get there by cab. You should probably call first and ask them if they've seen her. You don't want to go all the way there for nothing."

"Good idea." I click through to the restaurant's website and frown. "It looks like it's closed until five o'clock."

"So Laurel obviously isn't there," he says.

"I don't know," I reply. "I still feel like it's a possibility."

He groans. "How? The place is closed, Arden," he says. "Look, I know that you don't want to give up but—"

"Just let me call the restaurant, like you suggested," I interrupt him. "It's almost five o'clock, someone must be working."

"Okay, fine," Shep says with a sigh. "But if they haven't seen her then we're definitely giving up — for real this time. Agreed?"

"Mmhm," I say.

I hang up and immediately call Aijou but the phone just rings and rings. My chest tightens. Despite what I just promised Shep, I'm not quite ready to give up on the idea that Laurel could be at the restaurant. And even though I know that it's probably pointless to go and check, I'm going to do it anyway.

I text him as I hurry across the lobby towards the entrance: *I just need twenty minutes.*

My phone vibrates seconds later: *What happened to giving up?*

Give me twenty more minutes and I will. I swear.

I hold my breath, waiting for his response. I'm still going to go even if he insists on telling Andrew now, but it will make things a lot less stressful for me if he waits.

Twenty minutes and not one second more.

I smile. I send him the pinkie promise emoji and, before I can second guess myself, a heart.

I don't have time to mess around with public transit so I decide to take a cab. Fortunately, luck is on my side and there's a taxi idling outside the hotel. I hop in the backseat and give the driver the address, hoping that traffic isn't terrible and that thirty dollars is going to be enough to get me across town to the Distillery District.

As soon as we start to move, I send a group text to my parents and Riya to let them know that I think I might know where Laurel is and that I've gone to try and find her. *Please don't tell anyone the wedding's cancelled yet,* I add, and then I mute the conversation so I don't have to deal with them.

I try calling the restaurant a few more times as we crawl through the city, but no one answers. My heart is racing and I'm super anxious and I can tell that the driver is getting annoyed with me for constantly asking him if we're there yet.

My twenty minutes is almost up when we finally reach the restaurant. I thrust my last three ten-dollar bills at the driver and hop out, racing up to the building. I tug on the brass door handle but it's locked, which I guess isn't surprising considering that they aren't open yet.

My stomach clenches. I only have three minutes left. Three more minutes and Shep will tell his brother that the wedding is off. We just can't leave Andrew in the dark any longer.

I cup my hands and peer through the window. The restaurant is empty, of course, the tables set for the dinner crowd. The place is all dark wood and glass with a gorgeous cherry blossom tree set in the center, it's pink blossom-covered branches stretching towards the ceiling.

There's no sign of Laurel.

I frown. What am I doing? Did I really think that my sister would hanging out here eating sushi after running out on her wedding? That makes no sense. But then, I guess I don't really know what Laurel would do because I don't really know her. Not anymore.

I should have just let this go. I should have known that I can't fix this.

Crestfallen, I'm about to finally give up and try and find a subway station so I can make my way back to the hotel when I spot an older Japanese woman winding her way through the tables. I knock on the glass and she turns to look at me, then comes over and unlocks the door.

"Hi, I'm so sorry to bother you," I say, my face burning. I'm seriously going to ask her if Laurel is hiding somewhere in her restaurant?

It seems that I am.

I clear my throat. "I'm looking for my sister. This is one of her favorite restaurants and I just thought..." I stop myself. I sound ridiculous. The place is closed, Laurel obviously isn't here, I just need to move on.

But to my utter shock, the woman gives me a small smile and nods. "The poor thing was so upset I couldn't turn her away," she says. "I asked her if I could call someone for her but she said she just needed somewhere that she could be alone to think."

And then she holds open the door and gestures for me to come inside.

eighteen

IT'S PROBABLY NOT LAUREL, I tell myself as the woman leads me through the restaurant. *It's probably some other heartbroken girl who needed a quick break from her life. Don't get your hopes up.*

But I can't help it, my hopes are already up — like way, way up. My heart is pounding so hard that I'm having trouble catching my breath. The woman stops at the back of the restaurant and slides open a shiny black lacquer door, revealing a beautiful garden patio hemmed in by tall green hedges. She steps aside to let me walk past her and then discretely disappears, leaving me alone.

Or, as it turns out, not alone. Because as soon as I step around the corner, I spot my sister sitting at a rustic wood table, listlessly doodling something in her sketchbook. In front of her is a half-empty bottle of sake, a bowl of edamame that looks like it hasn't been touched, and a pile of crumpled tissues.

The rush of relief that goes through me is so powerful it makes my legs tremble.

"Laurel," I cry.

She looks up from her sketch and her puffy, red-rimmed eyes widen in surprise. "Arden," she says, her voice hoarse.

I run over and drop into the chair beside her, throwing my arms around her neck. My sister gives me a brief squeeze before pulling away from me.

"What are you doing here?" she asks, brushing a strand of strawberry-blonde hair off her forehead. She's not wearing any makeup and her skin is blotchy, her nose raw like she's been blowing it a lot. "How did you know where to find me?"

"I remembered that this is the place where you and Andrew went on your first date and I figured that I should check it out and here you are!" I shake her arm, still in shock that she's sitting beside me.

At the mention of her fiancé's name, Laurel's eyes fill with tears. "How is Andrew? God, he must really hate me for doing this to him."

I chew my lip. "Yeah, about that," I say. "He doesn't actually know that you've left him yet." I pull the envelope out of my bag and set it on the table. "I found your note and your ring when I went to your room this morning but I decided not to give them to him."

Laurel stares at the envelope like it's radioactive. "Why would you do that?"

"Because I wanted to talk to you first," I say. "I just wanted to make sure that you're really, really sure about calling off the wedding." I glance down the doodle on her napkin, a girl in a sundress on the bow of a ship, her arms thrown out, the wind rustling her hair.

"I guess I thought...well, I thought that since it's partly my fault that you're in this situation that I should at least try and fix it," I add. "So I told everyone that you had a migraine and then I spent the day running around the city looking for you. I figured that maybe you just had cold feet and needed some time to think and this way no would have to know that you almost cancelled your wedding if you changed your mind."

Except for Shep. And Riya. And my parents.

"Ardie, this isn't just cold feet," Laurel says, shaking her head. "And why on earth would you think that you're the reason why I'm cancelling my wedding?"

"Okay, I know that I'm not the only reason — dad told me what he said to you and I know all about Kaito and how he feels about you — but that terrible speech I gave last night certainly didn't help," I say. I pick up her hand and squeeze her fingers. "I'm so sorry, Laurel. I'm an awful maid of honor. Like the worst ever. I should have taken it more seriously, I should have listened to you and actually written a speech, but I didn't and then I decided to wing it and then I got drunk and panicked and it was a *total disaster* and—"

"Hold on," my sister says, holding up her hand and cutting me off mid-ramble. "You're right, you definitely should have listened to me about the speech — it totally sucked — but Ardie, that's not the reason I'm not getting married."

"It's not?"

She shakes her head. "It wasn't your speech and it wasn't what Dad said and it isn't Kaito—" Her eyes narrow. "Wait. How do you know about Kaito?"

"I met him at bookstore," I say and her eyebrows rise. "Riya mentioned you go there sometimes, so we thought we'd check."

"Who is we?"

"Shep and me." My cheeks start to burn just thinking of him. "He's been helping me look for you."

I suck in a breath. Shep. Oh my god! I forgot to tell him that I've found Laurel!

"Are you telling me that Riya and Shep both know that I've called off the wedding, but Andrew doesn't?" my sister asks as I whip my phone out of my bag. My stomach drops. I have six missed messages from Shep. I skim over the conversation — *Where are you? Why aren't you answering? Okay, I don't know what's going on, but you're out of time. I'm going to the apartment now.*

No! I quickly text him back. *L's here. I found her!!! I just need two more minutes!*

"Arden, hello? Can you put your phone down and talk to me, please," Laurel says, annoyed.

I glance at my sister. "You're right. I'm sorry," I say, setting my phone face down on the table. "But I wanted to stop Shep from going over to your apartment to tell Andrew what's going on. I told him to wait."

"Why?"

"So that you can tell him yourself."

Laurel pales. "I can't do that."

"Yes, you can," I say. "You have to. You can't dump him through a note, Laurel. That's heartless."

"I know," she wails, her face crumpling. "I know it's an awful thing to do but there's no way that I can face him.

He'll try to talk me into going through with the wedding and I just can't do that."

"But why?" I ask her. "If it's not because of Dad or me or Kaito, then why don't you want to marry Andrew? Don't you love him?"

"That's the hard part. I do love him. A lot." She grabs another napkin and blows her nose. "There's not just one reason that I don't want to get married, it's a bunch of little things that I ignored until I just couldn't ignore them anymore," she says. "I feel like I'm losing myself. Like a part of me is dying. And that's not how you're supposed to feel when you're marrying the love of your life."

"Is this about mom and dad?" I ask. "Because I totally get why their relationship would scare you off marriage." It's certainly turned me off the idea. "But just because they got divorced doesn't mean that you and Andrew will, too."

"It doesn't mean that we won't either." She glances down at her lap and starts to shred the napkin into pieces. "There was nothing you said in your speech last night that I didn't already know, Ardie. The chances of it actually working out for us when we're still so young are dismal," she adds. "Trust me, I've done my research, too."

I don't disagree with her, but I'm also still a little worried that she will regret her decision. Cancelling a wedding is pretty final — it isn't exactly something a relationship can come back from. Chances are this will mean the end of her and Andrew.

Then again, I'd much rather that she figure this out now then after she walked down the aisle.

"How long have you felt this way?" I ask her.

She shrugs. "Awhile," she says. "I guess I just got so

caught up in the excitement of planning a wedding that I didn't really think about what being married really meant." She looks at me. "There's so much that I'd have to give up — like first dates and first kisses. That moment when you lock eyes with someone new and you get butterflies."

I think of how I felt when Shep burst into the orchard with his dog yesterday afternoon, the way my whole body responded.

"And yes, I'd be gaining a lot, too, of course. I know that," Laurel says. "I know people search for years for their soul mates. And I might have found mine already."

It doesn't escape my notice that she said *might have.*

I swallow. "Are you sure this doesn't have anything to do with Kaito?" I ask. He *is* ridiculously hot.

Laurel shakes her head. "Kaito's a good friend, but I don't think of him in a romantic way."

We sit in silence for a moment as I digest everything that she's told me. There's definitely not going to be a wedding tomorrow. And while this might not be the ending that I hoped for when I set out to find my sister, I'm grateful that I got the chance to talk to her about this.

"Oh, I have something for you," I say, remembering Andrew's gift. I don't expect it to magically change her mind about getting married — at this point, I feel like she's making the right decision — but he did want her to have it. And so I take the box out of my bag and hand it to her.

"What's this?"

"Shep dropped this off for you at the hotel this morning," I say. "It's from Andrew."

Laurel runs her finger hesitantly over the cartoon sushi before she opens the box. When she catches sight of the envelope shaped locket, she lets out a long breath. "You're right," she says as a tear slips down her cheek. "I need to talk to him. I'll call him and ask him to meet me here."

A lump forms in my throat. I slide my arm around my sister's shoulders and give her a hug, wishing that I could somehow make this easier for both of them.

nineteen

"WHAT DO you think is going to happen now?" Shep asks me half an hour later as we walk down the cobblestone street, not headed anywhere in particular. I was happy to see him when he showed up with Andrew at the restaurant and even happier when he suggested that we leave and give Laurel and Andrew some much needed privacy. "Do you think they'll go through with the wedding?"

I shake my head.

Shep sighs and rubs the back of his neck. "This sucks."

"Yeah. It really does."

For Andrew but also for my sister. I know that it won't be easy, telling him that she doesn't want to get married.

Shep and I are silent for a few minutes as we walk, lost in our thoughts. I know that he's probably still angry with Laurel, that he might always be angry at her, and I can't blame him for that. She was careless with his brother's heart and that's a hard thing to forgive. I'd find it impossible if Andrew did this to my sister.

Shep sighs and stuffs his hands in the pockets of his

khaki shorts. "So tell me, Professor, did any of the Greek gods get a happy ending? Because I could really use one right about now."

Me too, to be honest.

"Well, the ancient Greeks aren't exactly known for their happy endings, but there is one story that is sort of romantic," I say as we stroll past a huge sculpture of a big red heart. We're still in the Distillery District, a trendy, pedestrian only area made up of old, industrial-looking brick buildings that have been converted into boutiques, breweries and restaurants. A ton of people are walking around, eating ice cream or taking photos.

"Oh yeah? Let's hear it."

"It starts with this King — his name was Polydectes — who hated his stepson, Perseus, so much that he decided to get rid of him."

"Are you sure this story has a happy ending?" Shep asks, nudging me in the side.

I smile. "Yes. I just have to tell you about all the murdering before we get there otherwise it won't make sense," I reply. "Anyway, like I was saying, King Polydectes hated Perseus, so he figured that he'd send him on an impossible quest, one that he'd never come back from — he tricked him into bringing him Medusa's head as a gift—"

"The lady with snakes for hair?"

I nod. "Also known for turning anyone who looked at her into stone."

"And the King wanted her head as a gift?"

"I mean, what he really wanted was for Medusa to turn Perseus to stone so that he didn't have to deal with him anymore," I say. "But much to King Polydectes' surprise,

Perseus managed to pull it off." I steal a glance at Shep and flush when I catch him stealing a glance at me. "Now we come to the love story: when Perseus was on his way home with Medusa's head in a bag, he saw the beautiful Andromeda chained to a rock."

We pass an old steam-clock. A man is taking a photo of his wife in front of it and Shep offers to take the picture so they can both be in it.

"Why was this girl chained to a rock?" he asks me after he's taking the photo and we start to walk again.

"She'd been sacrificed to the sea monster because her mother had bragged that her daughter was more beautiful than the sea-nymphs, which totally pissed the sea-nymphs off, and they were out for revenge," I say. "So Perseus comes by and spots Andromeda and instantly falls in love with her. He slays the sea monster and frees her, then he asks her to marry him."

"And they lived happily ever after," Shep says.

"Not quite yet. First, they had to deal with Phineas, the dude that Andromeda was supposed to marry," I say. "Phineas wasn't at all happy that she'd ditched him for someone else."

I shoot a nervous look at Shep. Laurel might not have dumped his brother for someone else, but this story still feels a little close to home. He doesn't seem to mind me telling it, though, because he just nods, encouraging me to continue.

"Phineas and his friends crash the wedding, intending to kill Perseus and force Andromeda to marry him instead, but the joke was on them because Perseus whipped out Medusa's head and turned them all to stone," I say.

"And *then* they lived happily ever after?" Shep asks, smiling hopefully at me.

I smile back at him. "Yes. Perseus and Andromeda got married and they had a long and happy life together. And when they died, they were placed into the sky as constellations."

"Cool," Shep says, but his attention has been drawn to an old red brick building. He comes to a sudden stop and stares up at the sign above the door and his expression turns somber.

"What's wrong?" I ask him.

"This is where the rehearsal dinner is being held," he says. "Was supposed to be held, I guess."

"Oh." My chest tightens. If this weekend had gone another way, then we would be in that restaurant right now, eating fancy canapes.

Shep looks over at me. "Do you want to go inside? I think that everyone is probably already in there. Minus the bride and groom, of course."

Right. I don't think the guests know the wedding has been called off yet.

"I don't know," I ask, chewing my lip. "What are we supposed to tell them?" Everyone's going to wonder where the happy couple is and I have no idea what to say. It's really not my news to share.

Shep shrugs. "We'll just say that Laurel and Andrew are running a bit late."

I'm not sure that excuse will hold up for very long — people are going to notice when they don't show up to their own rehearsal dinner — but okay.

We walk inside the restaurant. Laurel booked the place

for the entire night so everyone here is a friend or family. The place is Tuscan-inspired, with crumbling yellow stone walls and wrought iron everywhere, and it smells delicious, like simmering tomatoes and garlic. There's a harp player in the corner, set up near a table containing the groom's cake, which is shaped like a hockey stick, and a bunch of other really delicious looking desserts displayed on white china platters.

My stomach growls. It's been hours since I last ate anything and I'm starving. I start to head towards the dessert table, hoping to sneak a cookie or something, but my mom spots me and immediately runs over.

She hugs me tightly and hisses in my ear, "Where is Laurel?"

"She's with Andrew," I reply.

She relaxes and lets me go. "Oh thank god," she says, letting out a relieved sigh. "Everything is alright, then. Will they be here soon?"

"Um…"

"They're just running a bit late," Shep says, saving me from having to lie to my mother. It's a good thing, too, because if she found what's really going on, she would break down and then everyone would want to know why. And of course she'd tell them. She wouldn't be able to help herself.

Now that my mother thinks that the wedding is back on track, she looks down at my wrinkled sundress and inhales sharply. "Why are you still wearing this dress? And with those sneakers!" She shakes her head, exasperated. "Arden, this Laurel's rehearsal dinner! You know she specifically asked you to wear that beautiful pink skirt—"

"I didn't have time to go back to the hotel to change," I

interrupt her, suddenly self-conscious. Everyone in the room is in their finest, while Shep and I look like we've made zero effort on what is supposed to be one of the most important nights in our siblings lives. It's super embarrassing.

My mom frowns. I just know that she's dying to freak out on me about leaving the hotel without her permission — again — but she can hardly complain when I found Laurel, so she says, "You should have told me. I would have brought your clothes with me. Just imagine how this is going to look in the photos!"

It's not going to matter. Laurel might have hired a professional photographer for the evening — I can see him standing at the side of the room, snapping candid's — but I highly doubt she'll ever even look at the photos. Why would she ever want to remember this night?

Thankfully, my mom gives up on scolding me when she spots someone over my shoulder. She drifts off to talk to them, leaving Shep and me alone. My dad and Rachel are talking to Shep's parents. Riya, Nathalie and Charlotte are clustered together by the bar. Riya notices me and waves, but before she can come over, Shep reaches for my hand and pulls me around the corner and down a hall, just out of sight of the party.

We lean against the wall, our shoulders touching. My heart pounds. He's still holding my hand.

"We've made an appearance," he says, shifting to face me. "Now we can leave."

"Really? You think we should?" I start to laugh.

He grins. "I totally think we should. They won't even miss us."

I don't know about that.

Shep's eyes meet mine and I instantly turn all warm and melt-y. We move closer and closer still, until we're standing right up against each other.

"Arden?" he says quietly.

I swallow. This is it — he's going to kiss me. This is the moment that I've been waiting for all day. This is the point where we cross over from friends into something more.

And then, just as he dips his head, we hear cheering. We startle apart.

"Andrew and Laurel must have arrived," Shep says.

"What?" I'm surprised that they'd show up — I figured that after my sister told him that she doesn't want to get married that neither of them would be in any mood to party. Then again, they can't just leave all their guests hanging — they're still expecting a wedding tomorrow.

Shep and I hurry back into the main room. Laurel and Andrew are standing stiffly at the front. My sister's hands are clasped tightly together, Andrew's are jammed into the pockets of his khaki pants. Their eyes are red and swollen.

"Thank you all for coming tonight," Laurel says, her voice trembling. Everyone has gathered in a half circle around them. "We're so grateful for all the love and support that you've all given us over the years. Which makes it all the more difficult to tell you that Andrew and I..." She stops to collect herself then clears her throat. "Andrew and I have made the very difficult decision to cancel our wedding."

A collective gasp goes up from the crowd. My mom buries her face in her hands. Shep's father slides his arm around his mother's shoulders. They seem stunned.

"I know this comes as a shock to all of you, but I promise, this is the right choice for both of us," Laurel says.

Andrew has been staring at the ground since she started talking, but he suddenly looks up and moves a bit closer to her. He's upset — that much is obvious — but he doesn't seem angry. It makes me wonder if my sister was the only one having second thoughts.

"We're not sure what this means for us yet," Laurel continues. "And we ask for your patience and understanding as we figure it out."

"So maybe this isn't the end of them after all," someone whispers. I glance over and see that Riya has crept up beside me. She gives me a small smile. "We can only hope, right?"

I nod. I hope that Andrew and Laurel somehow make it through this, but regardless of whether they stay together or not, I'm proud of my sister for not buckling under the pressure to go through with the wedding — she stayed true to herself and that isn't an easy thing to do.

"Since we're all here, we hope that you'll stay and have dinner with us," Andrew says.

I frown. It's the only thing we can do, I guess, but the festive, party atmosphere is gone, replaced with a forced joviality as we all try to make the best of this super uncomfortable situation.

Andrew and Laurel immediately decamp to the head table, a blatant effort to avoid talking to anyone. The rest of the wedding party follows them. The harpist starts to play Can't Help Falling in Love — seriously? Did he not just hear Laurel's speech? — and we all make small talk but it's awkward. No one really knows what to say, so we're not really saying anything. And while the food is amazing —Panzanella salad with cubes of perfectly toasted bread and lots of fresh basil, green olives stuffed with almonds, thick, buttery noodles topped with mounds of fresh parmesan cheese — I'm suddenly not very hungry. Seeing Laurel and Andrew trying to put on a brave face has made me lose my appetite.

"I know great website where you can sell your wedding dress," Nathalie says to Laurel.

Riya pokes her hard in the arm.

"Ow. What?" Nathalie glares at her. "I'm only trying to help."

"Well, stop it."

We lapse into silence. Shep and I exchange a weighted glance. The muscles in my shoulders are knotted with tension.

I can't take this any longer.

And so I tap my fork against my water glass and stand up, my legs trembling as everyone in the room stares at me. Once again, I'm not prepared to give a speech and while I know that there's nothing I can say that will come close to making any of this better, maybe I can break the tension a little. Maybe I can stop people from casting sad glances at Andrew and Laurel all evening.

"Hi everyone." I give the crowd a nervous wave. There are way more people here than at the welcome dinner last night. Way more people to potentially embarrass myself in front of.

I can't believe I'm doing this.

"For those of you I haven't met yet, I'm Arden, Laurel's sister," I say, forcing myself to speak slowly and keep my breathing even. "I know this evening hasn't turned out the way any of us were expecting it to, but I just wanted to say that I think Laurel and Andrew are incredibly brave." My eyes sting as I look over at the two of them sitting side by side, their untouched dinner in front of them. "It took a lot of courage to make this decision and I'm so proud of both of you. And I hope that you realize just how much we all love you and that we're here for you no matter what. We're not going to let you go through this alone."

"Hear, hear," one of Andrew's friends calls out.

Everyone starts clapping in a show of support. Once it quiets down, I pick up my wine glass — filled only with water this time — my hands shaking slightly as I raise it into the air. "To Laurel and Andrew."

"To Laurel and Andrew," everyone echoes.

Glasses clink together. I sit back down, relieved that everyone has already gone back to their conversations and are no longer staring at me. Riya gives me a thumbs up and Andrew reaches across the table and fist bumps me, teary-eyed.

"Thank you," Laurel says, squeezing my hand.

It might not have been the greatest speech in the world — or the longest — but I got through it without humiliating myself, so I'll consider that a win.

Shep slings his arm around the back of my chair, his fingers grazing my shoulder. "Nice work, Professor," he says to me and my whole body lights up. "I was thinking, maybe I could show you more of the city once the party winds down."

There's literally nothing I'd like to do more, but given everything that's happened today, I should probably stay with my sister. She's going to need me. And Andrew is probably going to need him, too.

But before I can tell him that, Laurel leans over and says, "Go. Have some fun."

"What?" I ask. "Are you sure?"

She nods. "I'm sure."

"But what about Mom?" I ask her. There's zero chance she'll agree to let me go anywhere, not after what I pulled today.

"Let me worry about Mom," Laurel says. "You just worry about getting back to the hotel before midnight."

I smile. That I can do.

twenty

"HERE," Shep says, passing me something hard wrapped in a napkin as we sneak out of the restaurant half an hour later. It's mid-summer so the sun is still out but fortunately the air has cooled off a bit. "I noticed you didn't eat much so I snagged you a Nanaimo bar from the dessert table."

"Thanks," I say, smiling at him. I bite through the hard chocolate top and into the gooey soft custard. "Oh my god," I moan. "This is so good!"

"Right?"

I finish the whole thing as we walk through the Distillery district. We end up at the waterfront, strolling along a wide brick path that runs alongside Lake Ontario. Ahead of us, the CN Tower rises into the sky.

Shep seems a bit distracted, which I guess is only to be expected, given the emotional rollercoaster we've been on today. He catches me looking at him and he gives me a nervous smile, then takes my hand and leads me over to a quiet area off the path, near the trees. It's not private, exactly, but it's private enough that we won't be stared at while we're making out.

Shep slides his fingers into my hair and kisses me and it's every bit as amazing as I knew it would be. And, okay, I know that we live a million miles away from each other and it's impossible to imagine how this could ever work, but I want to try. I really want to try with him.

When we finally pull apart, Shep brushes a strand of hair out of my eyes. "This might sound crazy, considering that we've only known each other for a day, but do you believe in soul mates?"

I smile. According to Greek mythology, humans originally had four arms and four legs, as well as a head with two faces. Zeus feared our power so he split us into two separate parts, sentencing us to a life spent trying to find our other half. And while it's still way too early to know to whether Shep is my other half, I have a good feeling about us. I think we might be at the beginning of what could turn out to be a really amazing love story.

"I do," I say.

acknowledgments

Thank you:

Erin Cassone, Carla Cassone, Dallas DePagie, Dawn Dingman, Brooke Gilbert, Leiko Greaves, Sandy Hall, Brian and Joy Honeybourn, Sara Megibow, Pam Morrison, Stacie Palivos, Justyna Pyzowska, Missy Robinson.

And, always, Tony and Lila Stanic.

KING HENRY VIII won't shut up.

Not the real King Henry VIII, obviously. That would be crazy, given the dude's been dead for five hundred years. This King Henry is really Alan Rickles, retired weather-man/local dinner theater actor.

He's been talking to me for the past five minutes, although it should be clear from the platters of food I'm holding that I'm on my way to a table. My arms ache from trying to keep the heavy silver trays balanced— each one is weighted down with a rapidly cooling turkey leg, tiny pota-toes, and butter-glazed carrots, long green stems still attached. All of which our customers are invited to enjoy with their fingers instead of silverware, because knives and forks weren't used in the sixteenth century.

At least not in King Henry's court.

"Anne. Everyone always blames me for what happened to Anne," Alan says, sighing. "That's all anyone remembers me for."

Of course that's what we remember him for. Henry had

two of his wives beheaded. Not something people easily forget, even centuries later.

"What about all the good I did for England?" Alan strokes his thick brown beard. I'm convinced it's the reason he got the gig in the first place. That and the thirty extra pounds he gained for the role.

Yes. Alan gained thirty pounds to play King Henry VIII in a medieval theme restaurant in a strip mall outside of Seattle. Although I have to admit, in his fur- trimmed cape, heavily embroidered red tunic, and black velvet hat, he does look an awful lot like the portrait of Henry in my history textbook.

"I founded the Royal Navy, but do I get credit for that?" He shakes his head sadly.

"No one remembers the good stuff."

My wrists start to shake. I adjust the platters so the food doesn't slide off, hoping Alan will finally get the hint and let me go. I can't walk away from him— we're supposed to stay in character while out on the restaurant floor, and servants don't walk away from kings. Not if they want to keep their heads any way.

And I don't want to make an enemy of Alan. He's really into using his royal position to send the junior staff to the stocks, this vaguely fencelike contraption used as a torture device in the Dark Ages. Now employed in our restaurant for entertainment purposes.

Basically, you stick your head and hands through these holes cut in the wooden boards and then the boards clap down, trapping you. There's no lock, for liability reasons, but God help you if you try to get out before Alan has granted you a pardon.

Looking around in increasing desperation—seriously, my wrists are going to snap off— I spot Joe, my boss, standing near the stage. He's talking to a guy dressed as a pirate. People sometimes come here dressed in their sixteenth century finest, so at first I think it's just a customer channeling his inner Captain Jack Sparrow.

But then I notice the pirate is carrying the staff orientation manual. The manual is filled with strict instructions on dress code, suggested old-timey hairstyles, and medieval words and phrases we're meant to pepper our conversations with, like *I bid you, fare thee well* and, my personal favorite, *fie* —what passed for a swear word back in King Henry's time.

I'm too far away to tell what New Guy looks like— his face is partially obscured by an eye patch and the skull and cross-bones hat— but I'm hoping he's cute. We are in desperate need of some cute around here.

"Did I ever tell you about the time I was grievously injured in a jousting accident?" Alan leans on his gold-tipped walking stick. It's the posture he adopts whenever he's settling in to tell a long, drawn- out tale.

I nod, but I can't help looking over his shoulder at New Guy. Joe jabs a stubby finger at the stage, no doubt telling him not to go anywhere near it. I remember getting the same speech when I first started three months ago. Unless we are needed for a skit, something that thankfully doesn't happen very often, no one but Alan and Julia, the woman who plays Catherine of Aragon, are allowed on the stage.

The set consists of a tall red velvet throne placed in front of silver swag curtains. Alan spends most of his time sitting on that throne, quietly surveying the audience. Except, of course, when he's on the restaurant floor, trying to convince whoever is in earshot that Henry VIII got a bum rap and was simply misunderstood.

I'm hoping Joe will notice Alan has me trapped, but he heads in the opposite direction, toward the kitchen. New Guy follows behind him, his gaze roaming over the suits of armor standing at attention, the blue and red shields hanging from the fake stone walls.

"It happened during a tournament. I was thrown from my horse, you see," Alan says, squinting hard, like he's actually remembering something that happened to him and not to, you know, someone else entirely.

" 'Tis the reason I am now forced to use this." He waves his cane in the air, just missing Julia as she tries to sneak behind him. Before she can get away, I drop into a full curtsey. A few of the little potatoes bounce off the platters and onto the stone floor.

"Her Grace cometh," I say.

Julia scowls at me. Now that Alan knows she's there, she has no choice but to come over. Alan has even been known to send his queen to the stocks on occasion.

I give her an apologetic shrug before speed walking to table nine. Things have gone downhill since my last appearance ten minutes ago. The table is a mess, covered in broken crayons and the shredded pieces of a cardboard crown. The mother is mediating an argument between her two young sons over the remaining crown, while the father taps away on his phone.

"Here we go," I say, waiting for someone to clear a space on the table so I can set down their dinner. After it becomes apparent no one is going to help me, I give up and plop the platters on top of the mess.

The trays are barely out of my hands before the boys are grasping at the food. There are two turkey legs, one for each of them— their parents didn't order dinner; I guess greasy medieval food doesn't appeal to everyone— but the boys fight over the leg that is slightly bigger. Boy Number One manages to grab hold of it first, which results in Boy Number Two knocking him over the head with one of the foam swords sold in our gift shop. In the ensuing frenzy, a goblet— also sold in our gift shop—is sent flying. It's full of milk. Every drop of which lands on me.

Awesome.

The mother sighs—what can you do?—while the cold liquid seeps through the bodice of my velvet costume, right through to my skin.

" 'Tis no problem," I say. Wasted breath as no one seems to be worried that I'm now stuck in a wet costume for the rest of my shift.

I trudge back to the kitchen. Amy is scraping food scraps off a plate into a big green garbage bin by the dishwashing station. It's steamy and smelly back here, like old fried food.

"Table nine?" she asks, catching sight of me. She sets the plate on top of a towering stack of dirty dishes waiting to be loaded into the industrial dishwasher.

I nod, feeling miserable.

Amy passes me a rag.

"Cheer up. Only three hours till closing."

I dab at the stain but it's no use. The velvet has soaked up the milk and rubbing at it only seems to make it worse. Also, the fluff from the white rag is now sticking to the dark material.

Most nights aren't this bad. Most nights I actually like

working here. And not only because I need the money, although I do. I'm saving for the school band trip to London in the fall.

I've wanted to go to England since I was a kid and my gran would tell me stories about growing up in London after the war. She used to go back every year and she'd always bring the best stuff home for me—magnets shaped like Big Ben, a snow globe of Buckingham Palace. All kinds of British chocolate.

I can hardly believe I'll be there in a matter of months.

I'm still rubbing fruitlessly at the stain when Joe sidles up beside me. He's dressed in a green brocade long vest, black breeches, and shiny, knee- high black boots.

"Quinn. Excellent. I've been looking for you," he says, clapping a hand on my shoulder. "I'd like you to meet the newest addition to the Tudor Tymes team."

New Guy is beside him. He's a few inches taller than me, with wide shoulders that strain against his billowy pirate shirt. The eye not covered by the patch is a stormy gray. When he pushes the pirate hat back on his head and out of his face, I catch a glimpse of shaggy blond hair.

Definitely cute.

I smile at him, ready to welcome him to our strange little world, when he lifts the eye patch and I fully see his face.

"No need for introductions," New Guy says with a smirk. "Q and I go way back."

The smile freezes on my face. Because even though it's been five years and he's now taller than me and has a light scruff of facial hair, I recognize that smirk. Of course I do.

Wesley James.

Oh *fie.*

two

"YOU TWO KNOW EACH OTHER?" Joe's eyebrows lift in surprise. "Huh. Small world."

Yes. Too small. Way, way too small.

I glance warily at Wesley.

"I thought you moved to Portland."

He snaps the eye patch back over his eye. "And San Francisco. And Chicago. And Vegas," he says. "But my mom has always wanted to move back to Seattle, so . . . here we are. Again."

Here you are again, indeed.

I stuff the rag into my apron and glance at Joe.

"I have a table waiting. I should probably get back out there."

"Do me a favor and take Wesley with you," Joe says. "Show him the ropes."

Ugh, really? It's a struggle to keep the smile on my face, but I can't exactly refuse my boss. Not without explaining why. I don't want anyone to know my history with Wesley James, so I turn on my heel and lead him through the kitchen to the small bar tucked in the back. Bar may be a bit of a misnomer, since we don't actually serve alcohol. What we have is a soda fountain, an espresso machine, and a few gallons of milk tucked into a small glass- front refrigerator.

"So, Q. It's been, what? Four years?" Wesley watches as I grab a carton of milk and start to fill a plastic goblet stamped with the Tudor Tymes logo—a silver crest with a monogram of two interlocking Ts. I can feel him assessing me, marking the changes since we last saw each other. My hair is longer, but still blond and curlier than I'd like it to be. I also have a lot more happening in the chestal area than I used to, which, judging from the way Wesley's staring, he's definitely noticed. It makes me wish I had a sweater or jacket or something to cover up with.

I may look physically different, but I still feel the same inside. I still Hate. His. Guts.

"Five, actually," I say, sticking the milk carton back into the fridge. I set the goblet on a round silver tray along with a wicker basket lined with blue cloth.

"So fill me in. What have you been up to?"

What have I been up to? Hm. How to boil it down? Well, my parents got a divorce and my dad has pretty much been living like a nomad, bouncing from job to job. Still struggling with his gambling addiction, thanks for asking. Oh, and my gran, well, we had to put her in a home a couple of months ago. She has Alzheimer's. And all of this is your fault, Wesley James. Well, maybe not the part about Gran getting Alzheimer's, I guess I can't blame him for that. But he's definitely had a hand in everything else.

This isn't exactly the place to unload on him, though, so I just say, "Stuff."

"Stuff?" Wesley shakes his head. "Yeah, that really doesn't tell me anything."

Kind of the point.

I use a pair of tongs to pinch two rolls from under neath the heat lamp. There's a beat of silence while Wesley waits for me to hold up my end of the conversation. This is the part where I'm supposed to ask him what his life has been like, how he's spent the past five years. When I don't, he jumps back in, like I knew he would. Wesley never could stand silence.

"Well, I see one thing hasn't changed," he says. "You haven't outgrown your fascination with all things English." He catches the surprise on my face. "It's why you're working here, right?"

I nod, dropping the rolls into the basket. "I can't believe you remember that."

"I remember a lot of things about you," he says.

I remember things about you, too. And none of them are good.

Wesley reaches past me, grabs the rolls out of the basket, and starts to juggle them. Which is not only weird but completely unhygienic.

"How's your gran?"

The mention of Gran makes my heart squeeze. I guess that must show on my face, too, because Wesley stops mid-juggle.

"Wait . . . she's not . . . ?"

I shake my head. "Still alive." If you can call it that.

His face relaxes in relief.

"Great. You know, I'd love to see her. Catch up."

Not going to happen. Wesley's already taken so much from me. I'm not letting him have Gran, too.

"You know, juggling with the food is generally frowned upon," I say.

"Whoops. Sorry. Force of habit," he says sheepishly, dropping the rolls back in the basket.

I toss the soiled buns in the garbage and grab some fresh ones. Lifting up the tray, I push through the kitchen door and make my way, once again, to table nine. Fortunately, it's a slow night and I only have the one table to worry about.

The kids seem to have settled down, probably because they're stuffed full of nutritious, deep-fried turkey. I set the milk down in front of Boy Number One and place the basket in the center of the table. They didn't ask for more bread, but sometimes more bread is the key to getting a better tip. Or any kind of tip.

"How now." I bob a curtsey. "Prithee, I'd like to introduce—"

"Captain Grimbeard," Wesley interjects, extending his hand to give each boy a hearty handshake. They stare at him, awestruck. Clearly pirate trumps royal servant in the eyes of eight- year-old boys.

"Um, yeah. Anyway," I say.

"Captain Grimbread—"

"Grim*beard*."

"Captain Grimbeard is assisting me tonight. Pray tell, can I get thee anything else?"

It's like I haven't even spoken, these kids are so into Wesley and his stupid eye patch.

"You lads like magic?" Wesley reaches over and pulls a Tudor Tymes chocolate coin from behind Boy Number

Two's ear, a totally lame trick that somehow manages to delight the entire table. They erupt in applause like he's David Copperfield or something.

A few minutes later, I'm pushed aside while Wesley makes balloon animals—which, hello, they totally did not have balloons in the Middle Ages. And even if they did, they were probably sheep bladders or something, and they almost certainly didn't use them to make balloon animals.

When the trumpet sounds to signal the start of the show, I shepherd Wesley to the back of the room where the waitstaff are supposed to remain, hidden in the shadows. I guess this is to make sure that none of us distract the audience from the real show—i.e., Alan.

"So, you're, like, a pirate magician?" I whisper to Wesley as the lights dim.

He smiles. "Cool, huh?"

"That doesn't even make sense," I say. "Pirates don't do magic tricks. They rape and pillage."

"You're thinking of Vikings."

Clearly I need to bone up on my pirate history.

"Okay, fine. But I know for a fact that they didn't have magicians in the Middle Ages."

"Well . . . technically the king had fools—"

I can't help but smile.

"—but you're right, they were more like clowns than magicians," he says. "But who doesn't love magic?"

Right now? I'm not so fond of it. Unless, of course, Wesley's able to make himself disappear. That I could definitely get behind.

"I can't believe you're still so into it," I say. Wesley used to carry a magic wand with him everywhere. But that was when we were eleven.

He shrugs. "Some things stick with you."

I can't argue with that. After all, as he pointed out earlier, I've been borderline obsessed with England for years. That probably seems just as weird to him.

"Explain the balloon animals, then," I say. "Not something magicians normally do."

"I worked the birthday party circuit in Vegas."

"Wow. That's . . ."

"Geeky?" Wesley smiles. "Go on. You can say it. But I'll be

laughing all the way to the bank." He holds up a five-dollar bill and nods toward table nine.

I narrow my eyes and make a grab for the bill, but he holds it out of my reach.

"That's my tip, you ass! I earned it."

He folds the money into his pants pocket, where he knows I'm not about to go after it.

"Maybe we can work out an arrangement. Magicians always need assistants."

Is he kidding? He started working here *an hour ago*. As if I'm going to help him with his stupid tricks!

I cross my arms, fuming, as Alan waddles onto the stage and settles himself on the throne. He clears his throat and begins to deliver a somber Shakespearean monologue. Because this is Alan's idea of a show small children are dying to see.

"I come no more to make you laugh," he booms, tapping his gold-tipped cane against the stage floor.

"Things now, that bear a weighty and a serious brow . . .

sad, high, and working...full of state and woe . . . such noble scenes as draw the eye to flow."

Alan loves a dramatic pause, so it usually takes him forever to wander through this monologue. Surprisingly, no one ever leaves during his performance. Maybe they're afraid he'll throw them in the stocks.

"You go to West Seattle High?" Wesley asks.

"Yup." I glance at him, my stomach suddenly tight. "Don't tell me . . ."

He nods. "I'll be there in the fall."

Great. So not only do I have to work with Wesley, but he'll be haunting my school hallways as well. This night just keeps getting better.

"It seriously sucks to have to start a new school in my senior year," he says. "I kept in touch with a couple of people from elementary school, though, so at least I'll have a few friends." He nudges me with his elbow. "And you of course."

Is he for real?

Wesley James and I will never be friends.

Ever.

He takes in my crossed arms, the death-glare. And, finally, he gets it.

"Wait," he says, his smile fading. "You aren't still mad . . "

When I don't say anything, Wesley shakes his head. "Boy, Q. You can really hold a grudge."

He has no idea.

How can you still be mad? It was five years ago," he says. "And, when you think about it, I didn't even really do anything—"

"I don't want to talk about it," I snap. The words come

out louder than I expected them to, falling right into one of Alan's dramatic pauses. I sink back into the shadows before he can identify me—I'm hoping the stage lights mean he can't see the crowd clearly—and I don't breathe again until he resumes his speech.

As soon as the lights come up, I leave Wesley to fend for himself.

By the time I get home, it's nearly midnight. I text Erin—fortunately she's a night owl—and a few seconds later my phone rings.

"I hate my life," I say, collapsing on my bed. I really should have a shower—I stink like turkey and grease and despair— but right now I need to talk to Erin more than I need to be clean.

"You will not believe who I'm working with."

"Who?"

"I can't say his name. I'm too traumatized." I throw my arm over my eyes.

"Jason Cutler?"

Jason and I had a brief thing last semester. He dumped me over text the day before my birthday, so I understand why his name is the first to pop into her head. But while working with Jason would be heinous, it would still be preferable to working with Wesley.

"Worse," I say.

"Who's worse than Jason?"

"Wesley James."

"No! I thought he lived in Oregon?"

I sigh deeply and turn over, burying my face in my pillow.

"He moved back," I mumble.

"What are you going to do?"

I picture Erin in her room. It's twice the size of mine, with purple striped walls and a canopy bed, like something out of a fairy tale.

"What can I do?" I say.

"I don't know. Quit?"

"Not if I want to go to London. It's way too late in the summer to try to find another job. Besides, why should I quit? I was there first."

"Maybe it won't be so bad," she says.

"Maybe he's changed."

"No. He hasn't." I rub my eyes. I think I'm getting a migraine.

"Is he cute?"

"Erin."

"What? He was a cute kid. I'm trying to get a mental picture of what he looks like now."

"You don't need a mental picture. You can see him in person when he starts school with us in September."

"Seriously?"

"Why do you sound excited? This is the exact opposite of exciting news."

She laughs. "I don't know. Maybe because all you've talked about for years is what a jerk he is. How he ruined your life. I just think . . ."

"You just think what?" I prompt.

"Sixth grade was a long time ago, Quinn. People change," she says. "Maybe it's time to let go."

Erin doesn't get it. Wesley and his big mouth are the reason my parents are no longer together. That's not something I will let go of.

In the background, I can hear her fingers clicking the keys on her saxophone.

"You're practicing?"

"I'm not actually playing. My mom would kill me if I woke her up. I'm working on my finger technique."

Erin's very serious about music. I glance guiltily at my clarinet case leaning against the wall in the corner of my room. I haven't pulled it out since band practice last week. Mr. Aioki is forcing us to meet over the summer so we'll be ready for the tour, but we're also supposed to practice on our own, too. And

I never seem to get around to it.

"So, how much did you make tonight?" Erin asks.

I dig in my pocket and pull out a few wrinkled bills and some coins, along with the stinky milk rag I forgot to dump in the restaurant's laundry bin.

"Thirteen bucks." At this rate, I should get to London around my fortieth birthday.

I sit up and grab for the mason jar on my bedside table. It's nearly full, which makes me feel a tiny bit better. I know without counting that there's almost three hundred dollars inside. I like to wait until it's completely full before depositing the money into my account.

"Every little bit, right?" Erin says.

I stuff the money into the jar and the coins make a satisfying clink against the glass.

"Every little bit."

three

I FIND Caleb restocking the science fiction section. He's crouched down, sliding a stack of paperbacks onto the wide wooden shelves.

"Hey." I nudge him with my flip-flop and my clarinet case bumps against my leg.

"Hey." Caleb straightens the books so the spines are all perfectly lined up and then stands. He's wearing a green polo shirt and khakis with knife-blade creases running down each leg. It's not even a uniform, this is just the way Caleb dresses. Like a middle-aged man.

"You're early." He checks his watch. "Practice isn't for another half an hour."

Caleb is the other clarinet player in concert band. He's better than me—by a mile— but that's because he actually cares about playing the clarinet.

"I know. I thought I'd check out the travel section," I say.

He smiles. "Again?"

"I think I'll actually pull the trigger this time." I've been eyeing an art book on England. I haven't bought it though because it's superexpensive and I'm trying to pinch every penny I can. But I've decided I need something to cheer me up after last night.

"You can use my employee discount," he offers. "Twenty-five percent."

"Thanks."

Caleb tells me he'll meet me at the register and I wander to the other side of the store, where the travel books are kept. It's a small section tucked near the in-store café, so the whole area smells like roasting coffee and banana bread.

I set my case on the floor, grab England's Greatest Attractions from the shelf, and flop into a squashy yellow chair. Once I'm settled, I open the book to page 67, the place I always start. Big Ben. Looking at the photo makes my heart beat a little bit faster.

My grandfather proposed to my gran on Westminster Bridge, at the foot of that famous old clock, more than fifty years ago. It's the first place I want to go when I finally get to London.

I'm so busy going over the long list of things I need to see and how I'm going to accomplish all of them in the small amount of free time Mr. Aioki is allotting us, that I don't notice the black Converse sneakers at first. When I look up, it's straight into a pair of dark gray eyes.

Wesley is standing in front of me in a rumpled T-shirt, his blond hair all mussed like he's just come in from a windstorm. The sight of him unexpectedly sends a nervous jolt through me.

"Well, looky here," he says. He's holding a large takeout coffee cup.

"You're not supposed to bring food or drinks into this part of the store," I say.

The corner of Wesley's mouth lifts up, a half smile. For some reason I can't figure out, he seems to find me amusing.

"Q, you are way too uptight. What are they going to do? Kick me out?" He takes a sip of his coffee, like he's daring me to tell on him.

And you know what? I'm considering it.

"What are you doing here anyway?" I don't like that he's hovering over me—it's like it gives him the upper hand, somehow—so I struggle out of the squashy chair. "Are you following me? Because I'm pretty sure stalking is a federal offense."

"I'm not stalking you," he says. "I'm here to see a friend. I happened to be over there"—he points at the café—"when I saw you over here. Thought I'd say hi."

Oh.

"Okay, well. Hi." I lean down to pick up my clarinet case.

Wesley takes advantage of the fact that I've relaxed my guard and plucks the book from my hand.

"England's Greatest Attractions." He glances at me. I can't read the expression on his face, but I immediately feel defensive.

"It's research," I say. "I'm going to London. With the school band."

I have no idea why I'm telling him this. The less Wesley knows about me and my life, the better. He can't be trusted. He proved that a long time ago.

"Really?" He sets his coffee on the narrow arm of the chair, where it will almost definitely tip and spill all over the pale leather, and flips the book open. He paws recklessly through the pages, flipping past photos of Buckingham Palace and Stonehenge.

"Hm. Maybe I should join band. I'd love to go to England."

"Sorry." I snatch the book back, almost catching his fingers as I snap the cover closed. "Not possible. It's concert band. You have to audition to get in."

"Shouldn't be a problem," he says. "I play the tuba."

"You're kidding, right?" 'Cause it must be a joke. The Wesley I knew was way too cool to go near a tuba. He was more of a guitar or drums kind of guy.

He cocks his head. And there's that half smile again. "Nope."

I snort.

"Oh, you think that's funny? Okay. So what do you play?"

Crap. I really should think before I snort.

"The clarinet," I mumble.

Wesley makes a big deal of holding his hand up to his ear. "I'm sorry, what? I didn't hear you."

"The clarinet," I snap. "I play the clarinet. Which, as everyone knows, is much cooler than the tuba."

I march away but he trails after me. He follows me all the way to the front register, where Caleb is waiting. I set the book on the counter. Wesley's right beside me, all up in my personal space, so I turn around and hiss, "Why are you still here?"

"I told you. I'm here to see a friend." He extends his hand to Caleb and they do some weirdly complicated boy hand-shake that makes my heart sink. Wesley did mention he'd kept in touch with some of the guys from elementary school.

"So what's up, man? Did you get the job?" Caleb asks as he rings up my book. I hand him my debit card, trying to keep my expression calm. Inside, though, I'm a tornado. Because I know what's coming. I know exactly what Wesley will say next. And I can't think of a way to stop him.

"Yup. In fact Q and I work together," he says.

And there it is. Another secret spilled by Wesley James.

Caleb's eyebrows fly up into his hairline.

"You work at Tudor Tymes, Quinn? You never mentioned that."

It's not exactly something I go around broadcasting. Most of my friends don't even know, with the exception of Erin. I was teased in middle school, so I've learned not to give anyone any ammunition. Working in a medieval restaurant is just asking for it.

"I loved that place when I was a kid," Caleb says. "Which character are you?"

Wesley chuckles. "She's a wench."

"I am not a wench," I say, glaring at him. "I'm a royal servant."

"Please." Wesley drains his coffee. He shoots the empty cup over the counter and it sinks perfectly into the small metal garbage can behind Caleb. "She's definitely a wench. She wears a corset."

They both stare at me, like they're picturing me in it right now, which is totally humiliating. I cross my arms over my chest to block their view.

"Yeah, well, he's a pirate magician." I make a face like, isn't-that-the-stupidest-thing-you've-ever-heard, but Caleb doesn't catch it. He's busy shoving my book into a recycled tote bag.

"You're still doing magic, dude?" he says.

"Helps with the tips," Wesley mutters.

"You mean it helps you steal tips." I take the bag from Caleb.

"We should probably get going. I don't want to be late for practice."

"Yeah." Caleb takes off his name tag and slides it into his pocket.

"You ready?" he says to Wesley.

Wait, what?

"Wes is coming with us. He's thinking about buying my truck, so I told him to come for a test drive. You don't mind, do you?"

Mind? Of course I mind. But I don't know how I can tell Caleb that without seeming like a total freak.

And so that is how I end up wedged between them, Caleb on one side and Wesley on the other. I'm scrunched over on the bench seat as close to Caleb as possible, but Wesley's knee still somehow keeps brushing against mine.

"How come you're selling your truck?" I ask Caleb.

He grimaces. "The payments are killing me. And with London coming up . . ."

He doesn't need to finish the sentence. Europe is not cheap. Sure, the band is holding fundraisers to offset some of the cost, but each of us is still expected to kick in almost fifteen hundred dollars. Not all of our parents can afford it. Some of us have to sell our trucks or get jobs in medieval-themed restaurants.

We drive down California Avenue, past boutiques and coffee shops, bakeries and thrift stores, past a whole lifetime of memories. I let Wesley and Caleb carry the conversation

— mostly about horsepower and gas mileage, eventually segueing into a debate about the Seattle Seahawks that I don't even try to follow, until we reach West Seattle High. Caleb and I climb out and Caleb tells Wesley to pick us up after practice. So I guess I haven't seen the last of him today.

Our footsteps echo in the halls. It's so weird to be here in the summer, when the school is deserted. The walls are freshly painted, no flyers or posters to clutter them up. It even smells different. Cleaner.

We slip into the band room. Erin's at the back with the other saxophones. She smiles until she notices I'm with Caleb then she shakes her head. She doesn't think I should hang out with him so much, considering he likes me and I haven't made up my mind about him yet.

On paper, Caleb is perfect for me. There are a million reasons why I should like him. He's smart and responsible, he's not bad to look at. He plays the clarinet. We're a match made in band geek heaven.

But.

He does not make my knees weak. Or my heart race or give me butterflies or any of t hose other clichéd feelings you're supposed to have when you like someone. But I'm hoping that will change.

I'm almost finished assembling my clarinet when Mr. Aioki pulls the door closed and steps up to the podium. He taps his baton against the metal and lifts his arms. As the rest of the band members raise their instruments, I quickly place my reed against the mouthpiece and slide the ligature over the top to keep the reed in place, trying to ignore the annoyed expression on my band teacher's face.

The sound of Beethoven's March in D Major floods the room, pushing Wesley and everything else out of my mind.

Jennifer Honeybourn is a fan of British accents, Broadway musicals, and epic, happily-ever-after love stories. She is the author of several young adult novels, including Wesley James Ruined My Life, When Life Gives You Demons, Just My Luck and The Do-Over. She also writes middle grade books under the pseudonym J.E. Hailstone.